D1553028

"Dad—Stop It!"

Robin Fear raised his eyes to his father. Nicholas stood emotionless, no expression at all on his face. His eyes were shut.

"H-help—!" Mr. Bradley managed to choke out. His eyes bulged. His face turned purple. He gripped his throat with both hands, his mouth gaping open. "Can't . . . breathe . . ."

A shudder of fright swept over Robin. He stumbled into the room.

What's happening? he wondered.

What is wrong with Mr. Bradley?

Is my dad doing this to him?

Is my dad going to *kill* him?

Books by R. L. Stine

FEAR STREET
THE NEW GIRL
THE SURPRISE PARTY
THE OVERNIGHT
MISSING
THE WRONG NUMBER
THE SLEEPWALKER
HAUNTED
HALLOWEEN PARTY
THE STEPSISTER
SKI WEEKEND
THE FIRE GAME
LIGHTS OUT
THE SECRET BEDROOM
THE KNIFE
PROM QUEEN
FIRST DATE
THE BEST FRIEND
THE CHEATER
SUNBURN
THE NEW BOY
THE DARE
BAD DREAMS
DOUBLE DATE
THE THRILL CLUB
ONE EVIL SUMMER
THE MIND READER
WRONG NUMBER 2
TRUTH OR DARE
DEAD END
FINAL GRADE
SWITCHED
COLLEGE WEEKEND
THE STEPSISTER 2
WHAT HOLLY HEARD
THE FACE
SECRET ADMIRER
THE PERFECT DATE
THE CONFESSION
THE BOY NEXT DOOR

FEAR STREET SUPER CHILLERS
PARTY SUMMER
SILENT NIGHT
GOODNIGHT KISS
BROKEN HEARTS
SILENT NIGHT 2
THE DEAD LIFEGUARD
CHEERLEADERS: THE NEW EVIL
BAD MOONLIGHT
THE NEW YEAR'S PARTY
GOODNIGHT KISS 2

THE FEAR STREET SAGA
THE BETRAYAL
THE SECRET
THE BURNING

FEAR STREET CHEERLEADERS
THE FIRST EVIL
THE SECOND EVIL
THE THIRD EVIL

99 FEAR STREET: THE HOUSE OF EVIL
THE FIRST HORROR
THE SECOND HORROR
THE THIRD HORROR

THE CATALUNA CHRONICLES
THE EVIL MOON
THE DARK SECRET
THE DEADLY FIRE

FEAR STREET SAGAS
A NEW FEAR
HOUSE OF WHISPERS

FEAR PARK
THE FIRST SCREAM

OTHER NOVELS
HOW I BROKE UP WITH ERNIE
PHONE CALLS
CURTAINS
BROKEN DATE

Available from ARCHWAY Paperbacks

For orders other than by individual consumers, Pocket Books grants a discount on the purchase of **10 or more** copies of single titles for special markets or premium use. For further details, please write to the Vice-President of Special Markets, Pocket Books, 1633 Broadway, New York, NY 10019-6785, 8th Floor.

For information on how individual consumers can place orders, please write to Mail Order Department, Simon & Schuster Inc., 200 Old Tappan Road, Old Tappan, NJ 07675.

FEAR STREET®
R·L·STINE

FEAR PARK #1

The First Scream

A Parachute Press Book

AN ARCHWAY PAPERBACK
Published by POCKET BOOKS
New York London Toronto Sydney Tokyo Singapore

The sale of this book without its cover is unauthorized. If you purchased this book without a cover, you should be aware that it was reported to the publisher as "unsold and destroyed." Neither the author nor the publisher has received payment for the sale of this "stripped book."

This book is a work of fiction. Names, characters, places and incidents are products of the author's imagination or are used fictitiously. Any resemblance to actual events or locales or persons, living or dead, is entirely coincidental.

AN ARCHWAY PAPERBACK *Original*

 An Archway Paperback published by
POCKET BOOKS, a division of Simon & Schuster Inc.
1230 Avenue of the Americas, New York, NY 10020

Copyright © 1996 by Parachute Press, Inc.

All rights reserved, including the right to reproduce this book or portions thereof in any form whatsoever. For information address Pocket Books, 1230 Avenue of the Americas, New York, NY 10020

ISBN: 0-671-52955-2

First Archway Paperback printing August 1996

10 9 8 7 6 5 4 3 2 1

FEAR STREET is a registered trademark of Parachute Press, Inc.

AN ARCHWAY PAPERBACK and colophon are registered trademarks of Simon & Schuster Inc.

Cover art by Bill Schmidt

Printed in the U.S.A.

IL 7+

PART ONE

1935

chapter
1

Meghan Fairwood brushed her long, wavy, red hair off her shoulders and reached out to open her locker door. "Oh no," she murmured to herself. She lowered her textbooks to the floor and rubbed the dark stain on the starched cuff of her white blouse.

How did I get this stain? she wondered. Is it ink?

She bent down, pulled out her pencil box, and removed the fountain pen. The shiny blue Waterman pen was a gift from her parents for her sixteenth birthday. It was an expensive present. It cost nearly four dollars. But it had leaked ever since Meghan started using it.

She unscrewed the top and examined the silver point. Yes. Leaking again. Her new white sailor blouse ruined. I'll have to tell Dad, Meghan thought, returning the pen to her pencil box.

I hate to bother him about a pen. He's been so busy these days, so wrapped up in his new job. But the pen will have to be returned to the store.

She stood up and smoothed the front of the gray wool skirt that came down nearly to her ankles. The long tiled hall of Shadyside High School rang with happy voices, laughter, and the banging of locker doors. School had let out for the day.

Meghan turned to the end of the hall and saw two blond cheerleaders on ladders stringing up a red-and-white, hand-stencilled banner. She squinted to read the words: GO, TIGERS! 1935 STATE BASEBALL CHAMPS!

Well, not quite, Meghan thought, rubbing the black stain on her cuff. They still have to beat Waynesbridge to get into the tournament.

The left side of the banner fell to the floor. One of the cheerleaders screamed, grabbed for it as it fell, and nearly toppled off the ladder.

Some kids laughed.

The banner reminded Meghan of Richard Bradley, her boyfriend. She searched the crowded hall for him. He must have gone straight to baseball practice, she decided. That morning, Coach Swanson had announced that Richard would pitch the Waynesbridge game.

Was Richard nervous?

Not at all.

4

"Who *else* should pitch the big game?" he asked Meghan, so handsome, like a Hollywood star, grinning that toothy grin of his, his pale-blue eyes twinkling.

Richard is a little conceited, Meghan realized. But she wished she had his confidence.

She pictured him on the pitcher's mound, his curly, blond hair poking out from under his cap, leaning forward, his face so intense, the muscles in his arms bulging under the gray uniform shirt.

Meghan turned back to her locker. And realized that someone was watching her. A boy with straight, brown hair, solemn-faced, pale.

Robin Fear.

He blushed when Meghan raised her eyes to his and smiled at him. "Hi, Robin," she said cheerfully.

She didn't really know him. He wasn't part of her crowd. She didn't think he was part of *any* crowd. He always seemed to be by himself.

She knew that he lived in a big stone mansion on Fear Street at the edge of the woods. The street had been named after his uncle or grandfather or something. Meghan wasn't sure.

Robin had the locker next to hers. She always said hi to him. She thought he was kind of cute. She liked his dark, thoughtful eyes. He seemed so serious all the time.

Robin always blushed, pink circles forming on his pale cheeks. It must be hard to be that shy, Meghan thought.

5

She pulled open her locker, and a pile of magazines tumbled out over the floor. Movie fan magazines her friend Abigail had loaned her.

Robin bent to help her gather them up. "Do you—do you like Clark Gable?" he stammered, keeping his eyes on a magazine cover.

"Yes," Meghan replied, a little surprised. Those were the most words he had ever spoken to her. "I saw him in *China Seas* Friday night. You know. With Jean Harlow. Did you see it?"

Robin handed her the magazines. He shook his head. "I don't go to the movies very often."

Down the hall, the banner fell again. Some laughing boys grabbed it away from the cheerleaders and started to have a tug-of-war with it.

The cheerleaders screamed in protest.

Robin gazed down at the top magazine in Meghan's hands. "Bing Crosby," he murmured, recognizing the face.

"Do you like him?" Meghan asked. "Did you hear his program on the radio last night?"

Robin shook his head sadly. "My dad doesn't let me listen to music on the radio. He only turns it on to hear President Roosevelt's talks."

"How boring," Meghan replied.

"How's my girl?" a loud voice interrupted.

Meghan turned to see Richard grinning at her from down the hall. He wore his baseball uniform and had the maroon-and-gray cap pulled down over his blond hair. His cleats thudded heavily on the hard floor.

"Hi. I thought you were at practice," Meghan said.

His grin grew wider. "On my way. Do you want to study tonight?"

Meghan laughed. "Study what?"

Richard's eyes flashed. "I'll think of something!" he teased. Without warning, he bent down and kissed her on the lips.

Meghan hated when he did that. It was as if he owned her, as if he thought he could kiss her whether she wanted to or not.

The kiss ended quickly. She raised her eyes to see Richard glaring over her shoulder.

"What are *you* staring at?" He sneered at Robin Fear.

Robin blushed a dark red. "I—" His voice cracked.

Richard laughed. "You want to see smooching? Go to the movies."

"I—I wasn't staring," Robin choked out.

Richard stepped around Meghan. He reached out a big hand and flipped Robin's necktie out from under his V-neck sweater. He wiped his hands, using the necktie as a towel, grinning at Robin, challenging him to do something about it.

"Stop it, Richard," Meghan demanded, pulling his arm away. "You're not funny."

"Sure I am," Richard replied. "Catch you later, Meghan." He turned and clomped away, the cleats thundering on the floor.

Meghan watched him make his way down the hall.

7

She found herself thinking about how she liked him in some ways and didn't like him in others.

Richard was one of the heroes of the school. B.M.O.C. *Big Man On Campus*. That's what the school yearbook called him this year.

Meghan felt excited to be dating a guy as good-looking and athletic and popular as Richard. The two of them were like the king and queen of Shady-side High. In fact, they were voted King and Queen at the Spring Prom.

But now, as the school year drew to a close, Meghan didn't always enjoy being with Richard. She didn't like some of his loud, rowdy friends. And she wasn't happy about the way he treated her. Dropping by her house at all hours without calling first. Grabbing her and kissing her in the halls at school.

Richard disappeared around the corner. Meghan turned back to apologize to Robin.

"Oh!" She uttered a surprised cry when she saw that he was gone.

Robin trudged home, kicking a stone along the curb. He gazed up at the gray, overcast sky and thought about how it matched his mood.

I just want to die, he thought.

He replayed the scene in the hall again and again in his mind. Each time, he felt more embarrassed.

Meghan Fairwood was being nice to me, he told himself. She *wanted* to talk to me. After all these months of having side-by-side lockers, we were finally having a conversation.

And then I let that big palooka Richard make a fool of me.

When he accused me of staring at them, I stood there stammering like a dummy. And then I let him use my tie for a towel and I didn't say a word.

I didn't fight him. I didn't try to shove him away. I didn't even speak.

Why am I such a coward? Why am I so afraid?

Meghan didn't laugh at me. But I know what she was thinking. She probably felt sorry for me. Way to go, Robin. You've got the prettiest girl in school feeling sorry for you because you're such a whiny, little mouse.

He angrily kicked a clump of dirt onto the sidewalk. The sky darkened. He felt a cold raindrop on his forehead.

Perfect, he thought bitterly. Now I'll get drenched.

He stepped off the curb onto Division Street—and nearly walked into an oncoming streetcar.

The metal wheels scraped against the tracks. A horn blasted.

Robin leapt back. The bright red streetcar rattled past.

Shaking his head, Robin took a deep breath. Don't kill yourself, he scolded himself. He shifted his bookbag onto the other shoulder and took another deep breath, his heart pounding.

The near-accident shocked him from his angry thoughts.

Richard Bradley picks on a lot of guys. It was no big deal, he told himself.

9

He pictured Meghan once again. The way she smiled at him when he handed her the magazines.

I think Meghan likes me. I think she likes me even if I am a cowardly little mouse.

A few minutes later, he reached Fear Street. He turned and made his way on the grass along the side of the road.

Simon Fear's burned-out mansion rose up on the next block. The mansion had been beautiful before the fire destroyed it. That's what people said. Now, as Robin passed by, it stood black as a cinder, the roof caved in, gaping holes where the windows had been, still smelling of smoke. A stern, practical man, Nicholas had built *his* house out of stone, unlike Simon, his doomed great-great-grandfather.

"No fire will drive me away," Nicholas once told Robin. "I have reclaimed all of the Fear property. And I intend to hold on to it forever."

Robin picked up his pace when his house came into view. The broad shadow of the house fell over the lawn. Robin felt a chill as he stepped into it. The front windows were always curtained, shutting out the world.

Dad likes his privacy, Robin thought.

A crew of gardeners in work shirts and overalls were trimming the long hedge at the side of the sweeping front yard. One of the men tilted a thermos to his mouth and drank, narrowing his eyes at Robin.

Robin entered through a side door. The massive, double front doors were seldom used. Tugging his bookbag off his shoulder, he made his way through a narrow pantry. He crossed the big kitchen with its sparkling counters and polished floor and stepped into the front hall.

"Anyone home?" Robin's voice echoed off the marble floor.

Silence. The two maids had quit earlier in the week. Robin could never figure out why the servants never stayed for long. Was it because the house was so big and cold? Or was it because of the rumors about all the strange things that happened on Fear Street?

"Dad? Are you home?"

He hoped his father had gone out. He didn't feel like talking. He felt like shutting himself up in his room and thinking about Meghan Fairwood.

A noise from the library made Robin jump.

Was that music? he wondered. Some kind of chanting?

He crossed the hall, his shoes clicking on the marble floor.

Robin pulled open the library doors, peered into the room—and cried out.

"Oh no!"

chapter
2

Robin slapped a hand over his mouth and backed out of the doorway. Thick snakes of purple smoke curled through the room. And in the middle of the strange, swirling smoke, Robin saw his father—floating in the air.

Floating on his back. Hands crossed over his chest.

Floating in the purple smoke.

His eyes closed. The tails of his suit jacket drooping beneath him. His legs stretched straight out, black shoes pointing up.

Floating, floating. Floating so comfortably, so peacefully, as if on a cushion of air.

Chanting softly to himself.

Did he see me? Robin wondered, not daring to peer in again. Did he hear me cry out?

Robin pressed his back against the wall and waited for his breathing to return to normal.

Should I step back in there and ask him what he's doing?

No. Absolutely not.

Robin didn't really need to ask. He knew that his father's library was filled with books on sorcery and the occult, books on dark magic and the dark arts.

Robin had spent many hours poring through the books when his father was away. Ancient books, many of them yellowed and crumbling. Filled with strange drawings and diagrams that Robin struggled to make out. Chants and spells and long histories, some in languages Robin could barely read.

Did my mother read these books too? Robin often wondered.

He barely remembered his mother. She died when he was four. Her body was buried along with other Fears in the little cemetery cleared out from the woods the Fear family owned.

Sometimes Robin visited the grave with his father. Nicholas Fear would always stare down at the smooth white stone without speaking, his face emotionless.

Robin often wondered how different his life would be if his mother had lived. Would he still be this shy, this awkward—this lonely?

Robin heard his father's soft chanting from the

library. Still pressed against the wall, he shuddered. He couldn't force back his fear. Why was his father floating like that in the swirling purple smoke? What other powers did Nicholas Fear have?

These were questions Robin knew he could never ask him. Robin's dad was a cold, quiet man. Even when Nicholas tried to be warm and fatherly to Robin, Robin always felt at a distance from him.

Robin heard the front doorbell ring.

Then he heard a soft *thud* in the library. His father must have lowered himself to his feet.

He heard his dad cough. Because of the thick swirls of purple smoke? Then the doorbell chimed again.

Robin stepped away from the wall as his father strode quickly out of the library. Nicholas Fear was six feet tall and always stood stiff and straight, even when moving fast. He was needle thin, red-faced, and nearly bald, even though he was only thirty-four years old. His rimless eyeglasses made his brown eyes flash.

He turned to Robin. "When did you get home?" he demanded in his high, shrill voice.

"Just now," Robin replied, clearing his throat. He followed his father toward the front door. "I stayed a little late at school and—"

"The servants have quit," Nicholas interrupted. "Please answer the door for me." He straightened his gray wool suit jacket. He always wore a suit, even on weekends, even on vacations.

"Who is here?" Robin asked, hurrying to keep up with his father. Robin's father received few visitors at the house.

"I'm expecting some businessmen. From town," Nicholas replied. He tightened the knot in his navy blue necktie. "I have no idea what they want." He scowled. "Whatever it is, I'm not interested."

The doorbell rang again. Robin could hear men's voices outside. He stepped up to the double front doors.

Nicholas frowned. He scratched his red, bald head. "Show them into the sitting room, okay, Robin?"

"Sure, Dad."

Robin pulled open the heavy oak door. He saw four men at the doorway, all in brown business suits. They all removed their hats and lowered them to their sides.

One of the men stepped forward, smiling at Robin. He was a big, brawny man, nearly bursting out of his suit jacket. He had thick, curly, blond hair and pale-blue eyes that crinkled at the corners.

He stuck out a big, fleshy hand and Robin shook it. "Hello, young fella. I'm Jack Bradley. We have an appointment with Nicholas Fear."

"Th-that's my father," Robin said awkwardly. "I'm Robin Fear." He stepped back so the men could enter.

"Do you go to Shadyside High?" Mr. Bradley asked. His blue eyes scanned the vast front hallway.

"Yes, sir. I'm a junior," Robin told him.

"So is my son," Mr. Bradley replied, his eyes on the expensive British wallpaper. "Richard. Do you know Richard Bradley?"

Richard is his son? Robin thought. The embarrassing scene with Meghan played once again in Robin's mind. Richard and Meghan. Richard Bradley and Meghan.

"Yes, I know Richard," Robin said, keeping his voice flat, emotionless.

"Funny. He's never mentioned you," Mr. Bradley said.

Robin didn't reply. He led the four men into the sitting room. Nicholas Fear stood stiffly behind his enormous mahogany desk. He eyed the men suspiciously through his rimless glasses.

They nodded to Robin's father, each holding his hat in one hand in front of him. Jack Bradley introduced himself and then the other three.

Robin watched from the doorway. His father made no move to shake hands with the men. He stood stiffly behind his large desk chair, as if using it as a shield.

Dad hasn't asked me to leave, Robin told himself. So maybe I'll stay and see what this visit is about. He sank back against the door frame, just out of his father's sight.

"May we be seated?" Mr. Bradley asked, motioning to the black leather chairs that faced the desk.

"If you wish," Nicholas Fear replied coldly.

The four men sat down. They held their hats in their laps. Robin's father remained standing. His pale hands clenched and unclenched the back of his desk chair in noticeable spasms.

"It's certainly a beautiful day," Mr. Bradley said, glancing at the sunlight flooding in from the tall window. "We've been having a lovely spring. The tulips in my garden—"

"May I ask the purpose of your visit?" Robin's father interrupted.

Robin swallowed hard. Why was his father being so rude to this man?

From the doorway, Robin could see the back of Mr. Bradley's neck go red. The man cleared his throat. "We have come to make a request on behalf of the town of Shadyside," he said formally.

Nicholas nodded. He stared coldly at Mr. Bradley, waiting for him to continue.

Mr. Bradley cleared his throat again. "A few weeks ago, the four of us traveled to an amusement park in New York City called Coney Island."

"How pleasant for you," Robin's dad interrupted again. A sneer crossed his face for a second. "A vacation?"

The four men laughed. Polite, nervous laughter.

Nicholas frowned at them. He pulled out the tall leather desk chair and sat down.

"We believe that an amusement park like Coney Island is just what Shadyside needs," Mr. Bradley continued. "As you know, Mr. Fear, this town was hit hard by the stock market crash six years ago. We still haven't recovered. We still have many men out of work. The town has so little income."

Nicholas impatiently waved a hand to signal Mr. Bradley to stop. "Why have you come to me? I know nothing about amusement parks. Did you come to sell me a ticket to the Ferris wheel?"

This time, the men didn't laugh at Nicholas's sarcasm.

"We've come to ask you to give the town a section of the woods behind Fear Street," Mr. Bradley said, leaning forward, gazing intently at Robin's father.

"Excuse me?" Nicholas's face reddened even more. He narrowed his tiny, dark eyes at Mr. Bradley.

"We have received money to build a park," Mr. Bradley told him, speaking softly, so softly Robin could barely hear him from the doorway. "We would like to clear part of the woods and build the park there. It would mean so many jobs for people. And it would bring hundreds and hundreds of tourists to Shadyside. With your permission—"

"You don't have it!" Nicholas snapped. He jumped to his feet.

Robin was startled by how tall his father suddenly appeared, tall and angry. Nicholas grabbed a silver letter opener off the desk and gripped it like a dagger. His face turned a deep scarlet.

"But, Mr. Fear—" Jack Bradley started to protest.

"The woods belong to the Fear family," Nicholas said through gritted teeth. "They will *always* belong

18

to the Fear family, Mr. Bradley. I must ask you to drop your plans. And I must ask you to stay away from the Fear Street Woods, stay away from all of my property."

Nicholas raised the letter opener. He motioned to the door with it. "Good day, gentlemen."

Mr. Bradley stood up. The others followed. But they made no move toward the door.

"Mr. Fear, I must ask you to think about your answer," Jack Bradley insisted. "I will send over the plans for the park tomorrow. Perhaps if you study them . . ."

"Good day, gentlemen," Nicholas repeated, clenching his jaw. Robin could see the veins in his forehead throb.

"We will not take no for an answer," Mr. Bradley said sternly. "Please think about this. If you say no—"

Mr. Bradley stopped short. He staggered forward clumsily—and appeared to choke. He let out a sharp gasp and grabbed his throat.

Robin uttered a low cry of surprise as the other three men clutched their throats too. They all struggled to breathe, uttering loud wheezing sounds, twisting their heads back, their eyes wide in sudden terror.

Robin raised his eyes to his father. Nicholas stood emotionless, no expression at all on his face. He had the silver letter opener raised in front of him. Behind the rimless glasses, his eyes were shut.

"H-help—!" Mr. Bradley managed to choke out.

His eyes bulged. His face turned purple. He gripped his throat with both hands, his mouth gaping open.

"Can't . . . breathe . . ." one of the others whispered. He sank to his knees on the carpet.

A shudder of fright swept over Robin. He stumbled into the room.

What's happening? he wondered.

What is wrong with them?

Is my dad doing this to them?

Is he going to *kill* them?

"Dad—*stop* it!" Robin shrieked.

chapter
3

Robin saw his father's expression turn to surprise.

The letter opener fell from his hand and bounced on the thick carpet.

The four men sucked in deep breaths.

"Robin—I didn't see you there," Nicholas said. He made his way to the man on his knees and started to help him up. "Are you okay?" Nicholas asked, suddenly concerned.

Nicholas turned to Mr. Bradley. "Are you feeling okay? Can I get you a glass of water?" Nicholas kept glancing up tensely at Robin.

Mr. Bradley, breathing normally now, rubbed his throat. "I—I don't know what happened," he stammered. "It suddenly felt as if my throat closed up."

"The strangest thing," one of the others said, picking up his hat from the floor. "Mine too. I couldn't breathe."

"As if someone tied a *knot* in my windpipe," another one murmured.

Nicholas shook his head sympathetically. "I felt it, too," he told them. "Perhaps something in the air . . ."

Robin studied his father. Is he lying? Robin wondered. I didn't see *him* choking. I saw him standing there calmly with his eyes closed.

"I shall have to have this room checked," Nicholas told them. "It has been shut up for too long. Perhaps the windows should be left open."

The men straightened their suit jackets. Shaking their heads, still rubbing their throats, they followed Nicholas to the door. Robin watched their grim expressions as they nodded goodbye to his dad.

"I will not change my mind," Nicholas called after them. "Your amusement park must go somewhere else. It will never be built on Fear property. Never."

He slammed the door, muttered something to himself, and took a deep breath. Then he turned to Robin. "Must be something in the air," he murmured, a strange smile crossing his face. "Come help me open the windows, son."

Robin clicked off the radio. The yellow dial light faded out slowly. A Saturday afternoon. He had been half listening to a baseball game. The Washington Senators were losing to the St. Louis Browns.

But Robin felt too restless to concentrate on baseball.

He felt restless. And bored. And lonely.

He gazed at the textbooks piled on his desk across the room. And thought about writing his history assignment. A sweet-smelling breeze fluttered the curtains over his bedroom window.

I'll go out for a walk instead, he decided.

Walking in the woods behind his house had become his favorite way to pass the time. As he made his way through the trees and thick undergrowth, Robin would invent conversations in his mind. Conversations with kids he liked at school, kids he wished were his friends.

He made his way downstairs—and nearly collided with his father. "Where are you going in such a hurry?" Nicholas demanded, eyeing Robin sternly.

"Just for a walk. In the woods," Robin replied.

"You spend a lot of time there," his father said, studying him.

Robin felt his face grow hot. "I like it there."

"Me too," Nicholas said, a smile breaking out on his face. "Maybe I'll join you for a bit."

They went out the servants' door in back and crossed the broad back lawn to where the trees began. It had rained the night before, leaving the ground soft and moist. They stepped around sparkling pools of water, inhaling the spring-fresh air.

Nicholas Fear was always so solemn, so stern. But Robin saw his father change on the few occasions they walked together in the woods. His eyes grew wide with delight. The unfurling of fresh spring leaves on the trees, the bright, blossoming flowers made Nicholas smile.

"This is all ours," he told Robin, in a warm voice Robin seldom heard.

They walked in silence for a long while, listening to the soft wind shake the trees.

Robin had a lot on his mind. He couldn't decide whether or not to break the silence. His father was a difficult man to talk to, even when he was relaxed and enjoying himself.

Finally, Robin decided to say something. He took a deep breath. "Uh . . . Dad? I . . . well . . . Did you have to say no to those men?"

Nicholas stopped walking. He wore a light-gray wool sweater over a stiff-collared white shirt and a wide, navy necktie. Robin wondered why he so seldom appeared without a necktie.

Nicholas narrowed his eyes at Robin, waiting for him to continue.

Robin took another breath. His heart pounded. "It's hard to make friends, that's all," he blurted out. "Very hard. This will make it worse." He felt better, just getting the words out.

Nicholas swiped a gnat off his bald head. His face reddened even more than usual. He scowled. "Most people in this town aren't worthy to be your friend," he muttered. He started walking again.

Robin hurried to catch up. "Huh? I don't understand, Dad."

"You're a Fear," Nicholas told him gruffly. "You

24

must remember that, Robin. The Fear family stands apart in this town."

Robin gazed thoughtfully at his father. "Stands apart?"

"We always have," Nicholas replied. "We're not like the others. That's why my great-great grandfather Simon built his mansion out here in the woods, so far from town. That's why he bought this property, these woods. And that's why I built here, too."

"Because we're different?" Robin demanded, unable to hide his confusion.

Nicholas nodded.

"Do you mean we're *better* than the others?" Robin asked.

"Just different," Nicholas replied. His smile had faded. He gazed into the distance thoughtfully.

A crackling of twigs and leaves made them both jump. Robin turned toward the sound. He peered through the low, leafy tree limbs—and saw a brown overcoat. And then a dark hat.

A man. Moving quickly through the woods.

"Who is there?" Nicholas called sternly. Angrily.

Robin let out a gasp when he recognized the man. Jack Bradley. Carrying a long rifle.

"Who is there?" Nicholas repeated.

Startled by the angry shout, Mr. Bradley turned, spotted Robin through the trees, raised the rifle, and aimed it at him.

chapter
4

"No!"

Robin cried out. Swung his hands over his face as if to shield himself. Waited for the crack of the rifle.

Instead he heard footsteps.

Lowering his hands, he saw the tense expression on Mr. Bradley's face. Then he saw that the man didn't carry a rifle.

What was it? Robin stared hard. Mr. Bradley carried some sort of ruler, a surveying tool.

"You startled me, Mr. Fear," Mr. Bradley said, uttering a nervous laugh. His blue eyes caught the sunlight. He lowered the wooden measuring tool.

Nicholas snorted. He stared coldly through his glasses, his face turning scarlet. "Why are you trespassing here, Mr. Bradley?" he asked in a shrill, tight voice.

Bradley frowned. "Trespassing? I was surveying this lot, sir. I thought you received word that—"

"I thought I told you clearly," Nicholas interrupted. "I will not have any part of my woods destroyed."

Robin took a step back. He felt his stomach knot, his throat go dry.

Are they going to fight? he wondered.

Dad is taller. But Mr. Bradley is so big and brawny and muscular.

He could see the veins throbbing at his father's temple.

They won't fight, Robin assured himself. They're both gentlemen. They won't let this get out of control.

Nicholas stepped closer to Mr. Bradley, as if challenging him. "I will not have an amusement park in my woods," he said through gritted teeth.

Mr. Bradley didn't back up. "Perhaps the town council has other ideas," he said forcefully.

"What do you mean?" Nicholas demanded. He leaned forward, practically shouting the words in Mr. Bradley's face.

Robin took another step back. Was his father really planning to fight the man? Robin had seen his father's temper rage. But he had never known him **to** fight.

"My partners and I have petitioned the town

council," Mr. Bradley announced, keeping his eyes firmly on Robin's father. "We want part of the woods to be reclaimed by the town."

Robin saw the veins throb even harder at Nicholas's temples. He saw his father's hands clench into tight fists.

"The woods here should be enjoyed by everyone," Mr. Bradley continued, clutching his wooden measuring tool as if it *were* a rifle. "One man shouldn't be able to keep all this land for himself." He shrugged his broad shoulders. "Besides, the records aren't clear. You may not legally own the property after all."

Nicholas's mouth dropped open. His face turned as red as a tomato.

Robin held his breath and waited for the explosion.

Waited for the curses. The rage. The swinging fists.

But his father surprised him.

The two men glared at each other, nearly nose to nose, as if having a staring contest. Neither of them blinked.

Then Nicholas said softly, almost in a whisper, "We'll see."

That's all. Two whispered words.

"We'll see."

Then he spun around and walked away, heading back toward the house, walking erect, his long, thin legs taking big strides.

Robin stood frozen in his spot, still holding his

breath, watching his father move so quickly away. Nicholas never glanced back.

Jack Bradley glanced at Robin, as if seeing him for the first time. Then, without a word, he turned and disappeared into the trees, his brown overcoat swinging like a cape behind him.

Robin shut his eyes and waited for his heartbeat to slow to normal. Dad will never let them take his woods away, he thought.

Never.

He will find a way to keep the town council from obeying Mr. Bradley's wishes.

Grateful that the encounter between the two men had been so short, that no fight had broken out, Robin began to feel better. He took a deep breath. The air smelled sweet and fresh.

I need a long, long walk, he decided. He turned and made his way through the woods to a small trickle of a stream. Flecks of sunlight danced over the ground at his feet. The only sounds he could hear were the soft plop of his shoes on the mud and the gentle lapping of the water.

He glanced around. Where are the birds? he wondered. Why are there no birds in these woods?

It's springtime. Shouldn't they be busily building their nests and hatching their babies?

A cluster of purple and blue wildflowers bobbed in the soft breeze. Robin searched for butterflies. He couldn't see any. No white moths of spring. No insects or birds or animals of any kind.

How strange, he thought. I've spent so many hours walking in these woods. But I never noticed that until now.

He followed the gentle curve of the stream through the birch and cedar trees, his shoes sinking into the soft ground.

A cough made him stop. And hold his breath.

He heard another cough. The crackle of leaves under someone's feet.

I'm not alone, he realized.

Who else is back here?

Jack Bradley? Is he surveying this part of the woods, too?

He slid behind a wide, white trunk. And peered out.

At the edge of the stream, he saw the flash of copper-colored hair.

A girl.

She turned, squinting into the sunlight as if searching for someone.

Meghan!

Robin's heart began to pound.

Is she looking for *me?*

chapter
5

Meghan uttered a cry of surprise when she saw the figure step out from behind a tree. Squinting into the sun, she didn't recognize him at first.

Then the straight brown hair, the dark, solemn eyes, the burning, red cheeks came into focus. "Robin!" she called.

What is he doing here? she wondered, watching him approach. How did he find my secret place? She searched the trees to see if he was alone.

He smiled at her. A shy, awkward smile.

She smiled back. Realized—suddenly, surprisingly—that she liked him.

"Hi," Robin said, stepping up to the edge of the

stream. She saw mud caked over his brown leather shoes.

"Hi," she echoed, brushing back her hair. She straightened one shoulder strap of the green jumper she wore over a pale lemon-colored blouse. "What are you doing here, Robin?"

He pointed behind him. "Just walking."

Meghan felt the warm sunlight on her face. The stream sparkled as the light danced over it. "It's such a beautiful day," she said. "Do you walk in the woods often?"

Robin nodded. "It cheers me up." The red circles on his cheeks darkened.

Meghan narrowed her eyes at him. "You're . . . unhappy?"

He shook his head. A shock of dark hair tumbled over his forehead. "No. I mean . . . I just like it." He avoided her gaze.

He's so cute, Meghan thought.

She plucked up a tiny blue wildflower and sniffed it. "The woods cheer me up, too," she told him. "I like this little stream. The sound it makes. Like tinkling bells."

He nodded again. He opened his mouth to say something. Then changed his mind.

I wish he wasn't so tongue-tied, Meghan thought. He's just so shy. He acts as if he's never talked to a girl before.

She raised her eyes over Robin's shoulder. Was that someone stepping out of the trees?

No. A gust of wind shook the fresh spring leaves.

"Does the stream lead into the lake?" Meghan asked Robin. She bit her bottom lip. What a stupid question, she thought. He must think I'm really boring.

Why am I suddenly tongue-tied too?

Robin smiled at her. "Yes. There are a whole bunch of little streams that feed into the lake. I think I've followed them all."

He shoved his hands into the pockets of his brown trousers. "It is my backyard, after all," he added, brushing the hair from his forehead.

His backyard, Meghan thought. *His* woods.

She had almost forgotten that Robin's father owned these woods. Almost forgotten Richard's story about how Nicholas Fear was trying to keep his father from claiming part of the woods for the town.

Almost forgotten that Robin was a Fear.

Meghan thought about the terrifying stories she had been told about the Fear family. She had grown up in New Jersey. Her family had moved to Shadyside six years ago.

Meghan had been ten and didn't want to leave her friends. But her father had lost his job a few weeks after the stock market crash of 1929. The family had no choice but to move in with their Shadyside cousins and start life all over again.

And as soon as Meghan arrived, she began hearing the whispered stories about Simon Fear and his family. How they practiced the dark arts and evil sorcery. How neighbors heard strange cries and howls in the night.

Stories about people venturing into the woods and never returning. Stories about how no birds would settle in the woods because of the evil there.

Of course, the stories weren't true, Meghan told herself.

Every town has its legends about some evil place.

Gazing at Robin, so sweet, so shy, Meghan knew the stories about his family couldn't be true.

"Am I . . . trespassing?" she asked with a smile.

The question appeared to surprise him. "I guess," he replied finally. Then he added, "I'm glad." And blushed.

"Maybe your father wouldn't approve of me walking in his precious woods," Meghan teased.

Robin's expression turned serious. "I—I'm not like my father," he told her. "You've probably heard stories about my family. I'm not like them."

She nodded. She didn't know how to reply to that. She twisted a lock of red hair between her fingers.

"Would you . . . uh . . ." He hesitated, his dark eyes on the ground. Then he got his question out: "Would you like to walk to the lake?"

"No. I—" She started to reply. But a sharp stab of pain made her raise her hand to her eye. "Oh!" She uttered a startled cry.

"What's wrong?" he demanded.

"Something flew in my eye," she told him. She rubbed the burning spot, but the pain grew more intense. "Ow!" Tears flowed from the eye, down her cheek.

"Let me see," Robin said. "Must be a gnat or a mosquito."

Squinting with her good eye, she saw him step forward, frowning with concern. He placed a warm hand on the side of her face. Gently, he lifted the eyelid and examined it, bringing his face close to hers.

"It's just a speck of dust," he announced.

His finger touched her eye gently. "There. I've got it out."

She blinked several times. The eye still burned. Tears rolled down her cheek.

"I got it out. But you should wash it with some cold water," Robin said. "Do you want to come to the house?"

"No. I . . . well . . ."

He still had his hand on her face.

Once again, she realized how much she liked him.

This always happens to me, she thought. I'm going out with one guy—and I meet another guy that I really like, too.

Blinking the tears away, she gazed once again over his shoulder.

And saw a figure burst out of the woods and come running toward them.

"No!" she managed to cry—before the intruder grabbed Robin and roughly pulled him away.

"No! *Stop!*"

chapter
6

Robin felt strong hands grab his shoulders. Felt himself being heaved aside before he could even cry out.

He stumbled, but managed to stay on his feet.

"Hey!" Finally finding his voice, he spun around.

And stared at Richard Bradley, his face an angry red beneath his curly, blond hair. Hands tensed in fists at his side. Blue eyes wild. Body arched, like a cat with its back up.

Ready for a fight.

"Richard—stop!" Meghan's voice cut shrilly into Robin's ears. "Leave him alone!"

Robin felt his fear turn to anger. "Hey, Bradley— what's the big idea?"

Richard turned from Meghan to Robin. "You were kissing my girl," he accused.

"He was not!" Meghan cried.

Robin took a deep breath. He studied Richard's angry face.

Am I going to have to fight him? Robin wondered. *Can I fight him? I haven't been in a fight since kindergarten.*

Richard stared hard at Robin. His lips curled into a sneer. He raised his fists, challenging Robin. "I saw you," he insisted, breathing hard. "I saw you kiss her."

"No—" Robin protested. His voice cracked.

"He was *helping* me!" Meghan cried shrilly. "What is *wrong* with you, Richard?"

She stepped between the two boys, facing Richard, and thrust out both arms as if to shield Robin. "I had something in my eye, and he was helping me get it out," she told him.

Richard's scowl didn't relax, but he lowered his fists. He turned to stare at Meghan and studied her face, trying to see if she told the truth.

"It's true," Robin told him. He wished his heart wouldn't pound so loudly, nearly muffling his voice. "I—I was just helping her. She couldn't get the speck from her eye."

Richard brushed a leaf off the pocket of his red-and-brown flannel sport shirt. He tucked a shirt flap into his denim jeans, keeping his eyes narrowed on Robin the whole time.

Then, to Robin's surprise, Richard's expression softened. And he laughed.

"Richard . . . what's so funny?" Meghan demanded.

He laughed harder.

She stepped forward and shook his big shoulder. "Stop it! Why are you laughing?"

"The looks on your faces," Richard replied through his laughter. He grinned at Robin. "I was just kidding. I wasn't serious."

Meghan's mouth dropped open. "Huh?"

Richard slapped Robin on the back. "I knew you weren't kissing her. I just wanted to see your reaction." He shook his head. "You went white! You really did." He laughed some more, a high, shrill horse whinny of a laugh.

"Richard, it wasn't funny," Meghan said angrily.

"Sure it was," Richard insisted, grinning. He turned back to Robin and shook his big fist. "Did you really think I was going to let you have it?"

"I don't know," Robin replied.

Richard *was* serious, Robin decided. Now he's just covering up. He's pretending it was all a joke because he sees that Meghan is upset with him.

At least he didn't beat me up in front of Meghan.

It's time for me to leave, Robin decided. "I have to get home," he said. "See you at school on Monday."

"Bye, Robin," Meghan said. "See you Monday."

Robin turned and started to walk past them. He didn't see Richard stretch out his foot until it was too late.

"Hey!" Robin uttered a cry as he tripped over Richard's outstretched shoe. He sailed headfirst into the mud, landing hard on his elbows and knees.

Richard tossed his head back in another horse laugh.

Robin gazed up in time to see Meghan flash Richard a furious scowl. Then she bent and helped Robin to his feet.

"I think he's jealous," she whispered. Her lips brushed Robin's ear. A chill tingled the back of his neck.

Does she like me? he wondered. He brushed himself off. Pushed his hair back from his forehead.

"See you in school," Richard called in a mocking voice. "But not if I see you first!" Another horse whinny.

Robin ignored him and stomped away. Stepping into a thick tangle of trees, he stopped. And glanced back.

Through the swaying leaves, he could see them kissing. Richard had his arms wrapped around Meghan so that she seemed to disappear behind the big flannel shirt. Her face was tilted up to his, her red hair tumbling down over his sleeve.

Robin sighed, unable to force down his jealous feelings.

I think she likes me, he repeated to himself. But how can she like me *and* a big jerk like Richard?

He watched their kiss end. Richard kept his arms around Meghan. "How come I keep seeing you with Robin Fear?" Richard asked her.

Robin moved forward, straining to hear her answer. But a gust of wind made the leaves rustle, drowning out her words.

"Well, how did he find our meeting place?" Richard demanded.

"It was an accident," Meghan replied. "He was taking a walk. He didn't know it was our secret place."

Robin realized he had been holding his breath. Eavesdropping on their private conversation was more exciting than he could imagine.

But does she like me? he asked himself again. And again.

Does she like me?

"But why do you *talk* to that guy?" Robin heard Richard ask.

Meghan's answer stung Robin like a snakebite. "He seems so lonely," he heard her say. "I just feel sorry for him."

Robin ran home, ran through the tangle of trees and shrubs, jumping over rocks and fallen tree limbs, the woods a green-brown blur.

All a blur.

As if his eyes were covered with tears.

As if the world were a hazy, fuzzy place. All dark images. Not solid at all. A hazy, fuzzy place you could run through and not feel a thing.

Not feel a thing.

Not feel upset. Or angry.

Or disappointed.

Or . . . heartbroken.

Not feel anything at all.

A blur. That led Robin into the back of the house. Through the kitchen. Toward the front stairs that would take him to his room. Hoping not to see his father. Hoping to get up to his room where he could think. Where he could replay the afternoon, the scene with Meghan and Richard, replay it again and again.

Which is what he always did when he was angry or upset.

Lie on his stomach in bed, face buried in his pillow and torture himself, torture himself, replaying the pain again and again.

Only Robin didn't make it up to his room.

He stopped at the bottom of the stairs. Glanced into the living room.

The room in sharp detail now. His vision no longer a blur.

Everything as sharp as could be.

Robin lurched into the living room.

Dropped down onto his knees beside his father.

His father. On his back. Eyes staring blankly up at the pink crystal chandelier.

His father. Robin's father. Dead on the living-room floor.

chapter 7

"Dad!"

Robin grabbed his father by the shoulders of his suit jacket and shook him hard.

"Dad! Dad! Please!"

Was he breathing?

Robin pressed a trembling hand over Nicholas's nose and mouth.

No. Not breathing.

Dead. Dead on the living-room floor.

"Dad—no! Dad! Please, Dad!" The words burst out from Robin's throat and echoed in the vast living room.

He shook his father harder.

Nicholas's body felt so light in Robin's arms, so

light and fragile. Thin. And brittle. He shook it anyway.

Not thinking. Not seeing. Everything a blur again.

A blur of reds and purples.

"Dad? Dad?"

Purples?

Robin glanced toward the doorway that led to his father's study. A haze of purple smoke hovered around the door. Faint wisps of purple, rising slowly to the ceiling.

Purple smoke? Again?

Robin lowered his head to his father's chest. Pressed his cheek against the smooth fabric of his white shirt. And listened.

To silence.

No heartbeat. No *thud* of life.

Silence.

"Dad? Please—Dad?"

Wisps of purple smoke floated into the living room, carrying a sweet-sour odor. Spicy with a hint of decay.

"Dad?"

The purple smoke swirled, heavier, lower. Robin gazed up, saw it form a cloud over his father.

Nicholas stirred.

Groaned.

Opened his eyes.

"Dad?"

"Oh. Hello, Robin." His voice calm. Matter-of-fact.

"Da-ad?" Robin's voice broke. He still gripped his father by the shoulders. "You're okay?"

Nicholas raised his head and glanced around the room. "Yes. I'm fine," he replied. But his voice revealed a little uncertainty, a little surprise.

"Dad . . . you—you—" Robin stammered. He felt so relieved, so relieved his father was alive. So relieved, his chest felt about to burst.

He wanted to hug his father. Hug him and press his cheek against his.

But of course he never would do that. Except to shake hands, father and son never touched.

"What am I doing in here?" Nicholas asked, sitting up slowly. He shook his head, as if trying to clear it.

Robin noticed that the strange purple smoke swirls had vanished.

"I don't know," Robin said, raising himself to his knees. "I—I found you in here." He swallowed hard. "You weren't breathing. I—I thought you were . . . dead. What happened, Dad?"

Nicholas shook his head again. He pulled off his eyeglasses and squinted through them as if trying to see the answer inside them. Then he replaced them carefully and swept a hand back over his bald head.

He gazed up at Robin, still trying to focus his eyes. "I'm not sure what happened," he said softly.

Robin climbed to his feet. Then he reached out both hands and helped his father up.

Nicholas swayed unsteadily, looking as if he might fall back to the floor.

Robin helped him to one of the big, overstuffed leather armchairs in front of the stone fireplace. "You don't remember how you got here?" he demanded. "You really don't remember?"

Robin never questioned his father like this. But finding him dead—or near-dead—on the floor had been too frightening.

Robin *had* to know what was going on.

"I was practicing something," Nicholas revealed, staring into the dark fireplace.

"Practicing . . . what?" Robin demanded.

Nicholas didn't reply for a while. He stared into the empty fireplace, squinting and unsquinting his eyes, working his jaw.

When he turned to Robin, he had a strange, unsettled expression on his face. "Did you see your mother?" he asked, staring hard into Robin's eyes.

"Huh?" Robin's mouth dropped open in shock. "Mom?"

"Did you see her?" Nicholas repeated. He sounded frightened.

Robin's throat tightened. *Something is very wrong with Dad,* he thought. A chill of dread swept down his body.

"Dad," Robin replied softly, trying to keep his voice low and calm. "You know Mom has been dead for over twelve years."

"Did you see her?" Nicholas insisted. He glanced around the room, as if expecting to find her.

"No, Dad," Robin replied, feeling sick, fighting down waves of nausea. "No. I didn't see Mom."

Nicholas let out a long sigh. "I thought you might see her."

Robin swallowed hard. "She's dead, Dad. Remember?"

Nicholas nodded. "She may come back," he said, returning his gaze to the fireplace.

Robin gasped. "What did you say?"

Nicholas didn't seem to hear him. He shut his eyes, as if closing Robin out.

"Dad—what did you just say?" Robin insisted.

"She may be back," his father said, sighing, eyes still closed.

Robin started to say something. But a sound at the living-room door made him stop.

A rustling sound.

A cough.

Robin spun to the doorway.

"Mom?"

chapter
8

A veiled figure floated into the room, surrounded by swirls of purple smoke.

Robin gaped in amazement. In horror.

He heard a hiss escape his father's lips. "It is she!"

Nicholas Fear leapt up from the armchair and grabbed Robin's shoulders, squeezing so hard that Robin flinched in pain. "I've tried for so long," Nicholas whispered.

The figure floated closer.

Robin squinted to see it clearly through the swirling mist of purple.

He could see the outlines of a woman's skirt, dark and long, nearly brushing over the floor. Behind the curls of purple, he saw her arms, her tiny hands held

47

in front of her waist. Saw the long, dangling sleeves of a loose-fitting blouse.

She flickered and floated—like a flame, Robin thought. Like a purple flame. He strained to see her face.

Did she have a face?

A wide-brimmed hat hid her face from view.

The purple haze formed a veil over her. Veil over veil. She appeared to Robin as a shadow inside a shadow. A hazy figure in a fog of blue-purple.

"Mom?" he gasped.

Robin could feel his father pressing up behind him. He could hear his father's wheezing breaths, hear his racing heartbeat. Feel the tight grip of his father's hands on his shoulders.

"Yessss!" Nicholas Fear hissed again. "Yessss! It is Ruth! It is she!"

A chill made Robin's entire body shudder. Watching the shadowy, hazy form float across the room, he struggled to remember his mother.

Struggled to remember her face. Her smile.

He could draw up only a blank face surrounded by dark curls. Were her eyes blue or black?

He couldn't remember.

He couldn't remember her eyes, her smile, her voice.

He couldn't remember her laugh.

Couldn't remember anything at all, except for the dark curls. And the smell of lilacs.

Lilacs?

How was he supposed to remember?

She died when he was four.

But now she floated toward him across the living room. Floated inside a cloud of purple mist, for their reunion after so many years.

Her long skirt rippled as she floated. Her arms suddenly appeared to bend and flap like pennants in a strong wind. The wide-brimmed hat shimmered and bobbed, hiding her face from Robin.

What have you done, Dad? Robin thought.

Have you really used your sorcery to bring Mother back from the grave? Have you spent the last twelve years in that dark library of yours, poring over your books, chanting your spells, calling up your eerie, purple smoke—have you worked all these years to bring her back?

How did you do it?

No. Please don't tell me.

Robin really didn't want to know.

He had a sudden urge to run, to burst out of the room without waiting for the shadowy, shimmering figure to arrive.

But his father's grip held him in place.

And he realized his legs were paralyzed, his whole body frozen—in fear? In amazement? In simple curiosity?

"Yessss, Ruth!" Nicholas hissed.

The figure drew nearer, the long skirt silently sweeping over the floor. The sleeves of the blouse billowing. The entire figure billowing like a shadowy cloud.

Nearer.

Robin felt a wave of sharp cold.

The air around the approaching figure was frigid, heavy with chill.

Please turn, Mother, Robin urged silently. Please turn so I can see your face.

He shivered. Even his father's firm grip on his shoulders couldn't keep his body from shaking.

The cold swept over him. He had never felt cold like this before.

Not an earthly cold.

A cold from beyond the grave.

The coldest cold of all. The lifeless chill of death.

Please turn, Mother. I want to see you. I want to see your face.

The billowing figure floated nearer. And then, as if reading Robin's thoughts, she turned her head.

The purple fog swept away. The wide-brimmed hat slid back.

And Robin saw his mother's face.

Saw the gray-green bone of her rotting, mold-spotted skull.

Saw the black, gaping pits where her eyes had once been.

Saw her hollow, gap-toothed grin. Her jawbone hanging slack. Bits of dried black skin clinging to the hole where her lips at one time had smiled at him. Where her lips had kissed him.

No lips now. No mouth at all. Just rotting chunks of meat and bone.

THE FIRST SCREAM

"Nooooooooo!" A low howl of horror escaped Robin's throat.

And when he saw the fat, brown worm twist its way out of his mother's gaping left nostril, he shut his eyes—and screamed and screamed and screamed.

chapter
9

And woke up screaming.

His father was leaning over him, squinting down at him through his glasses, his thin lips pursed and dry. And a nurse stood on his other side, a pleasant-faced woman in a white uniform, black hair tucked under her uniform cap.

Robin cut off his voice in mid-scream. Felt the soreness of his throat. As if it were on fire. As if someone had scraped sandpaper over his throat, down to his chest. Scraped and scraped until he ached and throbbed and bled.

His chest heaved. He struggled to catch his breath.

He gazed up at his father's concerned face. Struggled to focus. Saw his father's bottom lip caked with blood. From chewing it?

"It must have been a terrible nightmare, son," Nicholas murmured, glancing at the nurse. "It must have been the worst nightmare yet."

Robin tried to reply, but could only croak.

A nightmare?

No.

This has happened before, Robin knew. Dad has tried his sorcery before. And succeeded only in frightening me.

And then called it a nightmare.

Hired a nurse and called it a nightmare. Paid her to say it was a nightmare, too.

As if a nightmare could be that frightening. As if a nightmare could be as frightening as the *truth*.

But Robin always played along. What choice did he have?

"You were in a deep sleep, young man," the nurse reported. Saying what she was paid to say.

"How . . . long?" Robin whispered. The effort sent stabs of pain up and down his throat.

How long have I been screaming? he wondered.

"Today is Monday," Nicholas replied.

Two days? Have I really been screaming since Saturday?

Why was I screaming?

Robin couldn't remember. It was the other part of his father's strategy. Did he hypnotize Robin and force the memory away? How did he erase the memory from Robin's brain?

Robin knew he'd been frightened—horrified.

Horrified enough to scream for two days. But he couldn't remember why.

"Are you feeling okay?" Nicholas asked softly, but without any real feeling. He leaned over Robin, studying his face, studying his eyes.

To make sure I don't remember? Robin wondered.

"I'm . . . okay," Robin whispered, his aching throat reminding him of his ordeal.

"I'll get you a glass of water," the nurse offered. She vanished from Robin's view.

He raised his head. His bedroom looked the same.

At least his bedroom looked the same. Nothing had changed—except something deep in the farthest reaches of his mind.

Something lost now. A nightmare lost in a nightmare. A nightmare that was true.

Nicholas shook his head. A practiced move. As if he'd been rehearsing his sympathy.

"What a horrible nightmare you must have had, Robin," he repeated. "Thank goodness it is over." He sighed. "I wish this didn't happen to you so often."

Me too, Robin thought bitterly.

"I must leave for a short while," Nicholas said. He sighed. "I have a new nightmare of my own."

"Huh?" Robin wanted to speak, but the pain was too great.

"The town council met this morning," Nicholas reported, unable to hide the anger in his voice. "They couldn't wait to vote on that Jack Bradley's proposal."

The park?

Robin's memory floated back. Floated . . . like a ghostly figure.

A ghostly figure Robin had seen somewhere. Recently.

A figure floating in a room. . . .

Where? He couldn't remember.

"They voted to take the woods from us, Robin," Nicholas continued bitterly. "One hundred acres. They voted to take one hundred acres of our woods to build their foolish amusement park."

"Sorry, Dad," Robin mouthed.

"We can't let them do that to our property—can we, Robin?" Nicholas demanded. "We can't let them take the woods from us."

He isn't really talking to me, Robin realized. He's talking to himself.

"I'll be back up here soon," Nicholas said, patting the covers over Robin's chest. "Get some sleep, son." He headed out the door. "You'll be okay. It was only another nightmare."

No, it wasn't, Robin thought, watching his father leave.

It wasn't a nightmare, Dad.

It was real.

It's always been real.

That's what is special about my life. My nightmares are always real.

Jack Bradley hoisted the coiled rope onto his shoulder. Then he lifted the metal case of surveying tools and called to his two helpers. "This way! Barney! Ken!"

Shielding their eyes from the glare of late afternoon sunlight, the two men, in denim overalls and work shirts, followed Jack into the trees. Barney, tall and bearded, carried two more coils of rope. Ken, a nineteen-year-old who looked about twelve, carried a bundle of wooden stakes.

Jack motioned for them to hurry. The sun was already lowering itself behind the tall trees. He wanted to finish before dark.

He wasn't superstitious. And he didn't believe the wild stories he'd heard since he was a child. But he didn't want to be in the Fear Street Woods after the sun set.

His work boots sank into the soft ground. The tools clanked inside the chest as he stepped over a fallen tree limb. "Mark it here," he instructed Ken.

The young man wrinkled up his face, as if he didn't understand the words. Then he slid one of the wooden stakes out from the bunch and, with the other hand, produced a small sledgehammer from the back pocket of his overalls.

"Here?"

Jack nodded.

Ken bent and pounded the stake into the ground.

"Are we going straight back?" Barney asked, scratching his beard.

"Yes. Straight back," Jack replied. "We'll get the depth measured first. Then we'll measure the width."

Barney shook his head. "Whew. A hundred acres. Nicholas Fear must be howling like a wounded dog."

Jack smiled. He tried to picture stiff, stern, dignified Nicholas Fear howling like a dog.

I can't believe the man's selfishness, Jack thought. We even offered to share some of the profits of the park with him. But still he refused to even listen to us.

Jack didn't really want to take the hundred acres by force. But what choice did the town have? So many people were out of work. The amusement park will get the town going again, Jack thought. Without it, Shadyside might not survive.

"This is a big job for three men," Barney said, tying one end of a coiled rope around the stake in the ground. "Do you think we can finish measuring today, Jack?"

Jack pulled off his black leather cap and scratched his blond hair. "We'll do what we can, Barney."

Jack had asked his son Richard to help out. But Richard was running around somewhere with that girlfriend of his, Meghan Fairwood.

Jack sighed. I don't see much of Richard these days, he thought. If he isn't spending time with that girl, he's busy practicing with his baseball team.

I've got to make a date with him, Jack decided. Just the two of us. Maybe we'll go fishing at that spot on the Conononka where we caught all those catfish.

As the sun lowered and the air grew cooler, the three men continued to measure off the acres. Ken pounded the stakes into the soft ground. Barney strung the rope, the back of his work shirt stained with sweat, despite the coolness of the afternoon.

Deeper into the woods, Jack spotted a narrow, trickling stream. He peered into the clear water, searching for schools of minnows, but didn't see any.

"Do we cross the stream?" Ken asked.

Jack nodded. "The stream will have to go," he said, following it with his eyes. "We'll have to fill it in. We can't have a stream in the middle of an amusement park."

The water trickled pleasantly, a musical sound. The three men followed along the bank for a short while. Jack stopped when he saw shoe prints in the muddy shore.

Shoe prints of at least three people. "Strange. I didn't think anyone came back here," he murmured.

"It's narrow enough to jump over here," Barney reported.

"It's real shallow. We can walk through," Jack told him, stepping into the stream. The water rose only halfway up his boots. "It doesn't get deep until it nears Fear Lake."

They waded across the stream, stringing the measuring rope with them. The sun lowered even more. The sky darkened. Their shadows across the mud were a deep blue now.

"Stake the spot there," Jack said, pointing.

Ken knelt and pulled out a stake.

As Jack turned toward the trees, he heard the hard clang of the sledgehammer.

And then he heard Ken scream.

"Nooooo! My foot! Nooooooo!"

Jack gasped and spun around.

And saw Ken shrieking in agony.

First he saw Ken's face, twisted in pain. Then he saw the wooden stake, sticking up through the top of Ken's boot.

"My foot! My foot!" Ken wailed. His hands flapped the air frantically, like the wings of a wild bird.

Around the stake, bright red blood puddled up onto the boot.

How did he ever do that? Jack asked himself. *How did he drive a wooden stake through his foot?*

And then the questions flew from his mind as he hurried to help the young man. He and Barney knelt beside Ken, urging him to be calm, telling him he'd be okay.

"Should we pull out the stake?" Barney demanded, his voice weak, trembling.

Blood seeped all around the stake, trickling down the leather boot.

"No. Don't remove it," Jack instructed. "It'll start to bleed too much. We've got to get him to the car. Get him to Shadyside General."

"It hurts . . . Ohhhh . . . The pain!" Ken cried weakly.

Jack and Barney hoisted him to his feet.

"Help him to the car," Jack instructed Barney. "Ken, lean on Barney. Don't put any weight on the

59

foot. Barney will drive you to the hospital. You'll be fine. As soon as they stop the bleeding."

"What are *you* going to do?" Barney demanded.

Jack shrugged. "Finish up. Leave the rope, okay?"

"But, Jack—" Barney protested.

Ken groaned.

"Get him to the car," Jack urged sharply. "I'm only going to work another couple of minutes. Then I'll get out of here."

Barney started to argue, but saw that Jack had his mind made up. He tightened his arm around Ken's waist and helped him back over the stream.

Jack watched them until they disappeared into the trees. Even after they were out of sight, he could still hear Ken's groans and cries of pain.

Ken isn't a clumsy boy, Jack thought, shaking his head. Ken has always been a steady, dependable worker. How could he do such a thing?

How could he be so careless as to smash a pointed wooden stake right through his boot and foot?

Jack shuddered, imagining how much pain Ken was in.

And then the itching started.

It began on his chest. A light tingling. Jack hardly noticed it at first.

When he became aware of it, he thought a few insects were crawling across his chest. He scratched at them through the front of his work shirt.

The itching grew sharper. More like insect *bites* now.

And it spread to his shoulders. Under his arms.

Jack dropped the surveying tool and scratched his arm. "Darned bugs!"

Have I walked into some kind of mosquito swarm? he wondered.

They crawled over his neck now, pinching, biting. The pain grew intense.

He plucked at his throat, trying to pull the insects off.

But to his surprise, he could find no insects.

His chest itched, tingling, throbbing. He tore open his shirt and scratched with both hands.

The itching circled his neck. Ran down his back. His legs trembled. He gasped for breath.

He bent to scratch his legs. Then rubbed his itching cheeks.

"I—I can't take this!" he cried out loud.

But the words were muffled because the inside of his mouth was itching now. And his tongue itched and tingled as if a thousand bugs were crawling over it.

"H-help . . ." Jack stammered.

He scratched at his throat. Rubbed his cheeks. Scratched his itching chest.

Scratched and clawed. Clawing the skin off his chest.

But the itching didn't fade.

"Ohhhhh . . ." A low moan escaped his itching throat.

His legs itched and throbbed and could no longer hold him up. He dropped to his knees. Moaning. Gasping to breathe.

He clawed the skin off his arms. Dark blood soaked through his shirt.

Scratching and clawing. Clawing frantically, like a crazed animal.

I can't stop! he realized.

Can't stop! Can't stop!

Am I going to claw off *all* my skin?

chapter

10

Meghan fastened the buttons on the front of her blue, wool cardigan sweater, then crossed her arms over her chest. She peered into the trees, impatiently pacing a few steps in one direction, then the other.

Where is Richard? she wondered.

I can't wait here in the woods much longer. The sun is nearly down.

She shivered. The air had grown wet and cold.

This was a foolish idea, she told herself. Meeting Richard here. Telling my parents I had to stay late at school.

And now Richard isn't even here.

She suddenly found herself thinking about Robin Fear.

Was it just because these were his woods? No. Meghan admitted to herself that she'd been thinking about Robin a lot.

About his dark, solemn eyes. His shy smile.

Sometimes she pictured the two of them, walking together in school. Or walking alone together by the river or through Shadyside Park.

Could I really break up with Richard? Meghan wondered. Can I break up with him so that I can go out with Robin Fear?

Her thoughts surprised her.

Why can't I ever make up my mind? she asked herself.

I thought I really cared about Richard. Now I'm not so sure.

A gust of wind fluttered her hair. The trees trembled. She suddenly felt as if a thousand eyes were peering out at her from behind the bushes and dark tree trunks.

Don't get carried away, Meghan, she scolded herself.

There's no one else back here by the stream but you.

But then two low shrubs parted. Meghan heard the hard crunch of shoes on the ground. And a dark figure came running out at her.

"Richard—where were you?" she cried, her voice more shrill than she had intended. "I've been standing here alone in the woods for over half an hour."

"Sorry," he replied breathlessly. He stepped up to

her and kissed her cheek. His forehead dripped with sweat. She guessed he'd run the whole way.

"Coach kept us late," he explained. "He said we were only going through the motions. He wanted to see some team spirit." Richard scowled. "How are we supposed to have team spirit if he keeps telling us how bad we are and keeps us late every day?"

Richard mopped his forehead with the sleeve of his sweater. He leaned down to kiss her again, but Meghan backed away.

She shivered. "I really have to get home. It's almost dinnertime. This was a dumb idea."

He frowned. "It wasn't my fault." He slid an arm heavily around her shoulders.

She started to protest, then changed her mind. His arm felt warm. She couldn't shake her chill. She pressed her cheek against his chest.

They started to walk. Richard was talking. Something about the baseball team and its coach.

Meghan didn't really hear. She gazed into the trees. Only shades of gray and black now. As if all the color had been drained from the world.

Feeling Richard's weight on her shoulders, she thought about Robin.

Robin and Richard.

"What are you thinking about?" Richard's voice broke into her thoughts. He removed his arm from her shoulders.

"Huh? Nothing," she replied. "Just listening to you. I guess I'm worried that I'm going to be late for dinner. Mom is going to ask where I was. And you know what a bad liar I am."

He chuckled. "You always start to stutter and stammer when you lie."

He stopped walking. She saw his expression change. He squinted into the gray. "Is that a deer over there? On the ground?"

Before Meghan could reply, he started trotting over toward it. "Hey!" Richard let out a cry as he suddenly tripped. He appeared to lose his balance, his feet flying up behind him, his arms shooting out.

He landed heavily on the ground. Meghan watched him sit up slowly, shaking his head. "A rope," he explained. "Look. Someone strung up a rope across here."

"No kidding!" Meghan exclaimed. "Why would anyone do that?"

Richard didn't reply. He appeared to be staring in the other direction. Staring at the dark form of a deer lying on the ground.

Meghan hurried up to him as he climbed to his feet. They approached the unmoving body slowly, walking side by side.

Meghan cried out first.

It wasn't a body, she saw.

Not a body. Not a deer.

Not a deer. Not an animal.

A human. A human skeleton.

A skeleton with the bones . . . the bones . . . the bones picked clean.

Even in the dark, she could see the rib bones,

poking up smooth and gray. She could see the bare kneecaps, the leg bones bent so that the skeleton appeared to be trying to sit up.

One bony hand gripped the top of the ribcage, as if holding the heart or scratching the chest. The other arm stretched over the grass. The hand held an object.

A shiny object lay near the skeleton. Gripped in horror, Meghan squinted harder. A tape measure?

"Ohhhhhhhh."

Meghan heard a long, low moan from beside her. She turned away from the skeleton to see Richard's face twisted in horror. Richard's eyes . . . filled with *tears*.

Richard's whole body convulsing in shudder after shudder.

"Richard? Are you . . .?" She lowered her eyes back to the skeleton.

And saw the head.

Not a skull. Not bare, gray bone like the rest of the body.

The head remained. The face. The hair.

A man's face.

Still there. The skin nearly as pale as the bones of the skeleton. The eyes staring straight up. The mouth twisted open in a silent, frozen shout.

The head.

Still whole. Still fleshy. Still there.

Meghan pressed her hands against her face. She tried to scream. But no sound came out.

She couldn't take her eyes off it.

Just a head on top of a skeleton.

A man's head on top of bones. As if a swarm of insects had attacked and eaten everything but the head.

The head.

Jack Bradley's head.

"Dad!" Richard shrieked, dropping to his knees. Reaching out one hand, reaching, reaching out to the head on top of the bones.

"Dad! Dad! Dad! Dad! Dad!"

Richard's screams burst over the hushed whisper of the swaying trees.

PART TWO

1935

chapter
11

Robin stepped into the square of golden sunlight on his bedroom carpet. He had been pacing back and forth in his room since breakfast.

Jack Bradley's head and skeleton had been found in the woods almost a week ago. Robin hadn't seen it. But he had read the newspaper stories.

And thought about it.

And dreamed about it.

The newspaper stories described it in such clear detail. Jack Bradley's head lying faceup in the grass. His mouth twisted open in horror. The head still attached to the neck bone.

And the rest . . . just bones. Sprawled on the grass. Picked clean.

71

As if there had been no skin, no muscles, no organs, no veins.

Where had that all gone?

Mr. Bradley had been dead for only an hour or two when Meghan and Richard discovered him. So where had the rest of him gone?

Robin thought he knew the answer. His theory kept him awake at night, and had him pacing his room on this Saturday morning.

The Fears hadn't attended Jack Bradley's funeral. Robin was relieved his father hadn't chosen to go. He knew that Nicholas would not be welcome.

Robin read in the newspaper that the funeral was one of the biggest in the history of Shadyside. Mr. Bradley was a very popular man. As a member of the town council and as the major builder of houses in town, he knew just about everyone.

Mr. Bradley's plans to build an amusement park were also really popular. Most people believed the park would save the town and make it a big tourist attraction.

The newspaper said that Jack Bradley might have been the next mayor of Shadyside. Police departments from all over the state were sending men to help investigate his bizarre death.

Was he killed by some kind of animal—or animals—in the woods?

Was he murdered by a human?

Was it murder at all?

Could he have contracted some strange kind of rapid, flesh-eating disease?

So far, the police were mystified. They hadn't a clue.

Pacing in his room, his hands cold, tightened into fists at his sides, Robin thought he knew the answer to the mystery.

It was Dad, Robin thought.

He didn't want to believe it.

But who else could have been responsible?

Robin couldn't stop thinking about the angry meeting between his father and Jack Bradley. He couldn't forget the furious expression on his father's face the day they came upon Mr. Bradley surveying a section of the woods.

Had Robin's dad warned Mr. Bradley then? Had Nicholas threatened him?

Robin couldn't remember his father's exact words. But he had seen his father's rage. And he knew how determined Nicholas was to keep the woods—*all* of the woods—as Fear property.

Did Nicholas Fear murder Jack Bradley?

Robin thought of the swirls of purple smoke. Once again he saw his father surrounded by the eerie mist in his library, floating, floating in midair.

Just a dream, Robin's father had said. It didn't happen. Another one of your nightmares, son.

But Robin knew it had happened. Robin knew that Nicholas had spells and magic. Robin knew about the old books in the library and the sorcery they contained.

Did his father use magic to murder Jack Bradley?

Robin stopped pacing. He picked up an old

wooden top from the corner of his desk. A small top, a childhood toy.

Thinking about his father, Robin squeezed the top in his hand. Squeezed it hard, until his hand hurt.

Then he heaved the top at the wall.

It thudded loudly against the pale-blue wallpaper, then bounced and rolled across the floor.

I *have* to know, Robin decided.

I *have* to know if Dad murdered Mr. Bradley. I *have* to know the truth.

He hurried down the long staircase. Through the dark living room, the drapes pulled tightly over the front windows.

He stopped outside his father's library. The door was closed tight. But Robin heard sounds inside.

Music?

No. A woman's voice.

Holding his breath, Robin pressed his ear against the door. The woman was crying. Or was she laughing? Her voice was high and tiny, like a child's.

No. Wait.

Robin struggled to hear. A high-pitched wail drowned out the other voice. Then Robin heard a third voice, deeper. A hoarse, smoky voice, whispering words he didn't recognize.

Realizing that he still held his breath, Robin let it out in a silent *whoosh*. What is going on in there? he asked himself.

He pressed his cheek against the door. Inside the library, the voices seemed to tumble and soar. At least three voices—all female. Maybe more. Crying. Moaning. Whispering.

And over those unfamiliar voices, Robin heard another. His father's voice, soft and distant. "Ruth . . . Ruth . . ." Repeating Roin's mother's name in a steady chant.

"Ruth . . . Ruth . . ."

Robin heard sharp laughter. A woman crying. A woman singing a tuneless melody.

What is happening? he wondered, gripping the doorknob. What is my father doing?

Should I go in and find out?

Yes, he decided.

He turned the knob, pulled open the library door, and peeked in.

chapter
12

Gripping the doorknob so tightly his hand ached, Robin leaned into the dark room.

And saw no one.

The voices—the crying, the chanting, the singing—all cut off.

Silence.

Robin uttered a startled gasp. His eyes were drawn to a yellow cone of light from a small table lamp. Beside the lamp, Nicholas Fear sat in a fat, brown leather armchair, a large book in his lap.

"D-Dad?" Robin stammered.

His father kept reading for a few seconds, then slowly raised his eyes to Robin. "Hello, son. I didn't hear you come in." He sounded calm, drowsy.

Robin took a deep breath. His mouth suddenly

felt dry, so dry he wasn't sure he could speak. He glanced quickly around the room to make sure the women he heard weren't hiding somewhere.

"Dad? I—I heard voices," he finally managed to choke out. "I mean—"

Nicholas closed the big book carefully. A cloud of dust rose up from it as he shut it. Behind the glasses, his eyes narrowed at Robin. "Voices?"

Robin nodded. "I heard someone laughing, I think. And someone singing."

Nicholas set the book down on the table beside the chair. "Maybe I was humming to myself. Sometimes I do that when I read."

"No. I heard several women's voices," Robin insisted. "And I heard you chanting."

Nicholas frowned. He studied Robin's face. "I hope you weren't having a bad dream," he said softly.

"No, Dad. I really—"

Nicholas raised a hand to cut Robin off. "As you can see, there's no one else in here. I've been reading quietly by myself for the past hour."

Robin opened his mouth to protest once again. But he realized there was no use arguing. The library stood empty now, except for the two of them.

"Why did you come in here?" Nicholas asked, rubbing at a small, dark stain on the leather chair arm. "Did you want to ask me something?"

"Well . . . yes," Robin replied awkwardly. "But I don't know if this is the time—"

Nicholas motioned for Robin to take the leather

armchair across from him. "Sit down, Robin. Are you sure you're feeling okay?" He crossed his long legs as he continued to study Robin's face.

"Yes. I guess." Robin lowered himself over the soft chair arm, then slid into the seat. "I wanted to ask you about Mr. Bradley," he blurted out.

Nicholas's eyebrows jumped. But the rest of his face didn't move. "What about him?" Nicholas demanded sharply.

"I . . . well . . ." Robin hesitated. How could he accuse his own father of being a murderer?

"Yes?" Nicholas asked patiently, scratching the knee of his gray wool trousers.

"I know you didn't like him," Robin started.

"It wasn't personal," his father interrupted.

"But I know you didn't want him to build his park," Robin continued.

Nicholas nodded. "That is the truth. And now I'm certain the park won't be built." His face revealed no emotion at all.

"But, Dad—" Robin took a deep breath. "Did you *do* something to Mr. Bradley? I mean, they found his body . . . and . . . uh . . . it was so strange . . ."

Robin's heart pounded. This is too hard, he realized. I never should have come in here. I can't ask my father if he's a murderer, if he killed Mr. Bradley in such a weird way.

Nicholas sat up. He leaned forward, bringing his face close to Robin's. He cleared his throat. "Robin, are you asking me if I had anything to do with Jack Bradley's death?"

Robin swallowed hard. He nodded. "Yes."

A strange smile spread over Nicholas's face. His eyes stared hard into Robin's. "Did I *murder* Jack Bradley? Is that your question?"

Robin nodded again. He felt his face go hot. His knees trembled.

Nicholas leaned even closer, so close Robin could smell his bay rum aftershave. "Robin," Nicholas whispered, "I'm going to tell you the truth."

chapter
13

A shiver ran down Robin's back. Maybe I don't *want* to hear the truth, he thought.

But he knew it was too late.

"Of course I was unhappy about Jack Bradley's plan," Nicholas began, speaking slowly, softly. He kept his eyes narrowed at Robin. "And of course I would do whatever I could to keep our woods, to keep him from building an amusement park on our property."

So you *did* kill him! Robin thought, shivering again.

"But I had respect for the man," his father continued. He scratched his bald head. "And I have respect for the law, Robin."

Nicholas shook his head, his expression changing

to sadness. "I was as shocked by Bradley's horrible death as everyone else. I hate to see a good citizen of Shadyside die such a gruesome and untimely death."

Robin stared back at his father. He didn't move. He felt his heart thudding in his chest.

The air suddenly felt heavy and cold. Robin felt chilled, as if he had been sitting in a deep freeze.

He realized that his father was waiting for him to reply. But Robin couldn't think of a thing to say.

The two of them stared at each other in silence for a few more seconds. Robin was the first to turn away. "Uh . . . thanks, Dad," he murmured awkwardly.

"Feel better about things, son?" Nicholas asked.

Robin nodded. "Yes. Thanks. I'll . . . see you later."

Robin stood up unsteadily. His legs felt rubbery as he crossed the room to the door. He turned to see that his father had picked up the old book again and was turning back to his page.

Robin stepped out into the hallway and closed the heavy door behind him. I *have* to get out of this house, he told himself. I have to walk in the fresh air—and think.

He pulled open the front door. Bright sunlight flooded the front entryway. He stepped out into the sunlight and made his way toward the street.

Do I believe my father? he asked himself.

Do I believe what he just told me in there?

Of course not.

* * *

Meghan was crossing Park Drive when she saw Robin across the street, walking slowly up to the school. She called to him, but he didn't seem to hear her.

"Hey—wait up! Robin—wait up!"

She started to cross, but a black Hudson rumbled by. The car was packed with kids she knew. Three of them rode outside, standing on the running boards. They all waved and shouted to Meghan.

She waved back, then trotted across the street to catch up to Robin. He walked with his head down, as if thinking hard about something. He wore a loose, white sweater over baggy, brown trousers. His dark hair fell over his forehead.

"Robin?" Meghan called. He's probably heading to Shadyside Park, she thought. The park stretched behind the high school, all the way down to the river.

She called his name again, and he turned around. She saw surprise on his face, and then a shy smile.

Meghan felt her heart begin to race. I really have a crush on him, she realized. A serious crush.

She had found herself thinking about Robin a lot. And now seeing him made her suddenly feel nervous, kind of fluttery.

"Hi," he called as she ran up to him. "I didn't see you." He kept his hands shoved in his pockets.

"What are you doing way over here?" she asked breathlessly.

"Just walking," he replied with a shrug.

One of her white knee socks had fallen to her

ankle. She bent to pull it up, then straightened the front of her long, plaid skirt.

She grinned at him. "But I thought you only liked to walk in the woods."

His expression turned serious. "I had to get away."

"I know the feeling," Meghan replied. "Sometimes I want to get as far away as possible. Sometimes I want to get out of my own skin." She lowered her eyes. "My parents don't get along. Sometimes their fights just drive me crazy."

Why am I telling him this? Meghan wondered, feeling embarrassed. He doesn't want to hear about my family life.

"I—kind of have family problems, too," Robin confessed.

They walked side by side past the parking lot toward the back of the building. Meghan saw seven or eight boys playing softball in a corner of the football field. A blond-haired boy ran to first base. The first baseman caught the ball and tagged him. And a loud fight began over whether he was safe or out.

"Do you like sports?" Meghan asked Robin.

The question appeared to surprise him. "No. Not really," he replied, watching the kids shout and shove one another. "I like to listen to baseball games on the radio sometimes. But I don't like to play sports."

They walked past the field, making their way to the broad, grassy area where Shadyside Park began.

White moths fluttered over the grass. A robin tugged at a fat, brown worm.

"I'm a pretty good tennis player," Meghan said, trying to keep the conversation going. "That's really my sport. They make us play field hockey in gym all the time. I think it's so boring. I'd rather play softball or something. But of course, girls can't play that sport."

Why am I jabbering on and on like this? she asked herself. She felt so jittery, not at all like herself. And I'm not usually such a chatterbox, either, she thought.

It's Robin, she decided.

I'm trying to impress him. I'm trying to make him like me. To get his attention.

But it's so hard. He's so . . . shy. So deep inside himself. It's so hard to know if he even hears me.

They stopped in front of two old oak trees. The limbs overhead were twined together, forming an arch. The narrow dirt path led through the arch.

Does Robin like me? Meghan wondered. Does he think about me at all?

And suddenly, impulsively—*crazily*—she put her hands on the shoulders of his sweater, raised her mouth to his, and kissed him.

A short kiss. But a kiss.

Nice, she thought, her hands still pressed on his shoulders, his sweater warm from the sun.

"Oh!" He uttered a soft cry of surprise. His dark eyes went wide.

What have I done? Meghan asked herself.

She stepped back.

As a figure came leaping furiously toward her.

"Richard!" Meghan shrieked, seeing his angry glare. "Where did *you* come from? I just—"

Richard uttered an angry growl, like an animal about to attack. "Meghan—I don't believe you!" he cried. "You sneak out with—with *him* while I'm mourning my father?"

"No—" Meghan shouted. "You don't understand. I—"

She didn't get a chance to finish.

Richard uttered another animal cry. Then he swung around hard. His fist came up. And made a hard *thock* as he thrust it at Robin's face.

Meghan gasped as Richard's fist glanced off Robin's cheek and nose. A smear of bright blood washed over Robin's cheek, dripped onto his chin.

"Richard—stop it!" she cried.

Robin staggered back, stunned. His hand went up to his bloodied face. "Hey—" he choked out, more of a grunt than a cry of protest.

And Richard hit him again. A hard blow to the stomach.

Robin gasped. Blood spilled from his nose. He doubled over.

Richard grabbed his shoulders. Kicked him hard in the side.

"No! Richard—stop!" Meghan shrieked.

He ignored her cries. Kicked Robin again.

Robin let out a squeal. Covered his bleeding head with both hands.

"Stop it!" Meghan wailed. She grabbed Richard's shoulders, tried to pull him off Robin.

Richard swung his arm hard, sending Meghan toppling back.

He drove a hard punch into Robin's throat.

Robin gurgled. Blood puddled under him.

"Stop it, Richard! Stop it!" Meghan shrieked. "Stop it! You're going to *kill* him!"

chapter
14

Pain shot through Robin's chest. His stomach heaved. He struggled to breathe.

Covering his face with both hands, he felt blood, a river of blood, sticky and warm.

A blow to the chest made him groan. The pain felt like a sharp knife in his side. Or a whip. Someone cracking a whip against his ribs.

This can't be happening, he thought.

This can't be happening to me—in front of Meghan.

He rolled away from another punch. Somehow pulled himself to his feet. His legs trembled. His whole body shook.

I didn't fight back, he thought, still shielding his face.

I just let him punch me, kick me. I didn't fight back.

In front of Meghan. I didn't fight back.

She was helping him up, he realized. He lowered his hands from his face and saw her holding on to his arm. Her red hair had fallen in wet tangles over her face. She was breathing hard, trembling.

In anger? Or fear? Robin wondered.

He saw Richard behind her, calmly examining a cut on his fist. Richard didn't glance up.

"Are you okay?" Meghan asked in a whisper. "Robin—should I get help?"

He swallowed hard but didn't answer her.

I've never been so embarrassed, so humiliated, he thought.

I just want to die. To disappear.

I didn't fight back. I didn't fight back.

Meghan had to help me up.

"Nooooooo!" A long howl of protest burst from his throat.

And suddenly, Robin was running. Running from the park. Running past two startled boys on bikes who had to hit their brakes. Running past the softball game where another argument had exploded.

Running.

If only I could run away from *myself,* he thought.

If only I could run forever.

The phone on the end table in the living room rang. Meghan trotted in from the hall to answer it.

The heavy, black receiver had sticky stuff on the mouthpiece. Someone must have been eating something and talking on the phone at the same time, she figured.

"Hello?" Meghan said breathlessly.

"Hi, it's me." Richard's voice. "I called to apologize. You know. For this afternoon."

Meghan sighed. "Richard," she scolded, "you know I'm not allowed to talk on the phone. We have a party line. There are four other families who use this number. So I'm only allowed to talk in emergencies."

"Well, this is an emergency," he replied. "I didn't mean to lose control this afternoon. It's just that—"

"I really can't talk," Meghan snapped. "Sorry." She replaced the receiver.

Meghan still felt too upset to accept Richard's apology. She really didn't want to talk to him.

Poor Robin, she thought.

Richard is so big and athletic. He had no business picking on Robin like that. Robin didn't stand a chance.

Meghan couldn't chase away her guilty feelings. It was all my fault, she realized. If I hadn't kissed Robin . . .

Two minutes later, the front door opened. Meghan looked up from the book she was reading to see Richard burst into the house without knocking. "Why did you hang up on me?" he demanded.

"I told you. I'm not allowed to talk on the phone."

She slammed the book shut. "What do you want?" she asked coldly.

"To apologize," he said. "I know I shouldn't lose my temper like that. But sometimes I just can't help it."

Meghan rolled her eyes. "Some apology."

Richard crossed the room to her. He tried to take her hand, but she yanked it away from him.

"I saw you kissing Robin Fear, and that's what set me off," he said.

Meghan nodded. She knew it had been her fault. "But you nearly killed him, Richard," she said, softening.

Richard tugged back a strand of his blond curls. He pressed his lips into a pout. "I'm really sorry," he said. "Please don't be angry at me."

He looks like a little boy, Meghan thought. She realized she still was attracted to Richard.

"Well . . . maybe I'll accept your apology," she said coyly. She stuck out her hand. They shook hands.

"You don't really *like* Robin Fear—do you?" Richard demanded.

Yes, I do, Meghan felt tempted to say. But she was afraid of setting off Richard's temper again. And she really didn't want to hurt him.

So she ignored the question. "Why were you in the park, anyway?" she asked, rubbing at a dirt spot on one of her brown-and-white shoes.

"Just stay away from him," Richard warned. "I

mean it. I'm apologizing for what I did. But stay away from him, Meghan."

"Why were you in the park?" Meghan repeated.

"I was looking for you," Richard replied. He pulled up a leather ottoman and sat down across from her. "I had good news. But then I saw Robin and . . ." His voice trailed off.

"Good news?" Meghan leaned toward him, propping her head in her hands. "What kind of good news?"

"It's about the park," Richard said excitedly. "The town council—they voted to claim a section of the Fear Street Woods for the town. In honor of my father's memory."

"Richard, that's wonderful!" Meghan cried. She jumped to her feet, clasped her hands together, and raised them over her shoulder in a sign of victory. "Yaaay!"

"Yes," Richard agreed. "It means that the amusement park will be built. My father's dream will come true."

Meghan cheered again.

Richard raised both hands to quiet her. "That's not the only good news, Meghan. I've got more. The mayor called my mother to tell her the whole plan."

"What *is* it? What plan?" Meghan demanded.

"After all the trees are cut down," Richard said, "the town is going to hire as many kids as possible to chop up the stumps. Girls, too!"

"Really? Girls, too?"

Richard nodded. "They're going to pay us a dollar a day—and free admission when the park opens."

Meghan whooped for joy. She hugged Richard.

I'll be able to earn some money this summer, she thought. A dollar a day! I'll be able to help out Mom and Dad.

"I can't wait for my dad's dream to come true," Richard said happily. "I can't wait for the park to open."

"Neither can I!" Meghan cried, letting out another joyful whoop. "I can't wait, either!"

She had no way of knowing just how long—and horrifying—the wait would be.

chapter
15

"Can you meet me after school?"

Meghan turned away from her locker to see who had whispered to her. "Robin? Hi."

She slammed the locker door. Then turned back and studied his face. "Are you okay?"

Robin rubbed the small, purple bruise on his right cheek. "Yes. I'm hunky-dory. Fine." He blushed.

It was Tuesday afternoon. Meghan hadn't seen him since that horrible fight on Saturday. "You don't look bad at all," she told him.

"The bruises were mostly mental," he replied, lowering his eyes to his scuffed, brown leather shoes.

Remembering Richard and his threats, Meghan glanced up and down the long hall. "Richard doesn't want me to talk to you." The words burst from her mouth before she could hold them back.

Robin shook his head. "Does he really tell you who you can talk to and who you can't? Do you let him do that?"

"Of course not," Meghan answered quickly. Now it was her turn to feel embarrassed. "Where shall I meet you?" she blurted out.

"In the woods?" Robin suggested. "At that meeting place by the stream?"

Meghan shook her head. "No. I won't go there," she told him. "Not since . . . we found Richard's father nearby. I—"

"How about Roger's?" Robin asked. "We can get a malted or an ice cream soda. I'll treat."

He seemed so eager. Almost desperate.

Does he like me? Meghan wondered. Even after I got him beat up?

Roger's was a drugstore with a long soda fountain, a hangout for Shadyside High students, just a couple of blocks from the school.

What if Richard comes in and sees us? She couldn't keep the question from her mind.

No, she decided. The baseball team has a game after school. Robin and I will be safe.

"Okay," she whispered. "I'll meet you there at four."

She slammed her locker shut, turned, and started away just as Richard came around the corner. "How's my girl?" he asked loudly.

"Just fine," Meghan replied, and kept walking.

* * *

Meghan pushed open the glass door to Roger's and found Robin already waiting for her in the last booth behind the soda fountain counter. The place was crowded with noisy, laughing kids, drinking tall malteds and sharing ice cream sundaes, eager to blow off some steam after school.

"Hi," Robin called, motioning for her to sit down across the small table from him. As Meghan slid into the red leather booth and dropped her book-bag on the floor, she saw that his expression was solemn.

"What's wrong?" she demanded.

Before Robin could answer, the white-uniformed waitress stepped up, pad in hand, to take their order. They both asked for chocolate malteds.

Two friends waved to Meghan from stools at the counter. Meghan waved back, then returned her attention to Robin. "Is everything okay?" she asked. "You look so troubled."

He raked a hand tensely through his dark brown hair. "I really wanted to talk to you," he said.

She smiled at him. "Well? Here I am."

She felt disappointed that he didn't smile back.

A song started up on the radio. Meghan recognized it, a jazzy Cab Calloway scat number called "The Jumpin' Jive."

She suddenly felt like jumping up from the booth, grabbing Robin, and dancing. Instead, she leaned over the table so that she could hear Robin over the music.

"My father is an evil man."

Was that what Robin said? Meghan strained to hear over the blaring radio. "What did you say?" she asked.

Robin leaned closer. Now their faces were only inches apart. "My father is more evil than anyone around here knows," he told her.

Meghan drew back, startled by Robin's words. She thought he had asked her here because he wanted to ask her out on a date.

Why was he telling her about his father?

Robin must have read her thoughts. "This is about the amusement park," he explained. His dark eyes burned into hers. "I'm trying to tell you. My father is furious that they took away part of the woods. And he's furious that they're starting work on the park."

The waitress set down the malted milk shakes in their tall glasses and a bowl of whipped cream to dab on top. Robin waited for her to leave before continuing.

Meghan plunged the straw into the malted and took a long sip, still wondering why Robin was telling her all this.

He ignored his malted and leaned over the table to talk to her. "I want to escape my father's evil," he continued.

"Huh?" Meghan wiped chocolate off her chin with the napkin. "I'm not following you, Robin," she confessed.

"I want to show my father that he has to stop

using his evil powers," Robin said urgently. "I want to show him that he can't control people's lives."

Meghan shoved the glass aside. "What are you going to do?"

"I want to join the work crew on the park," Robin replied.

Her mouth dropped open. "Huh?"

"The crew of teenagers," Robin explained. "They're going to hire teenagers to chop up all the tree stumps to clear the woods. And I want to be on that work crew."

Meghan felt a stab of dread. "But, Robin," she said softly, "if your father finds out—"

"He won't find out," Robin interrupted.

"But what if he *does* find out that you're working against him?" Meghan demanded. "What if he does find out you're working to build the park? What will he do to you?"

Robin frowned. "I'll sneak out," he replied. "He'll never know."

Meghan reached across the table and squeezed his hand. When she started to pull her hand away, he held onto it. He wrapped it between both of his hands.

"I—uh . . . well . . ." He hesitated. Then the words burst out of him in a fast-flowing stream. "I— I really like you, Meghan. You probably already guessed it. I think about you a lot. I'm joining the work crew mainly so that I can see you."

His words surprised Meghan. And pleased her.

She raised her eyes to his and saw that he was waiting for some kind of reply. "I'd like to see you, too," she told him.

The answer made him smile. He still held on to her hand. His face was so close, she could see her reflection in his dark eyes.

Once again, she felt drawn to him. Once again, she leaned forward and kissed him.

And then she dropped back against the seat with a sigh. "Are you sure you want to be on the work crew?" she asked him. "I'm worried, Robin. I have a bad feeling about it. A very bad feeling."

Robin's eyes flashed. "Don't worry," he said. "I can take care of myself. My father won't do anything to me."

chapter

16

School had already been out for a week. Meghan couldn't wait for the work crew to begin. She knew that chopping up stumps was going to be hard work. But it would also be fun with dozens of other young people around. And she'd be earning enough money to help out her family—and save up for some new clothes for the next school year.

She showed up at the work site in the woods wearing a floppy, blue cap pulled down over her hair, a baggy pair of denim overalls, and a pair of her father's work boots. She felt strange not wearing a skirt. Strange being outdoors in men's clothes.

But when she saw other girls wearing slacks and overalls, she started to relax. As she approached the cleared area of the woods, the sound of chopping hatchets floated out to her. Eager to pick up that dollar a day, some kids had gotten an early start.

She had signed up for the crew before school ended. Now she joined the line of kids signing the day's work sheet, picking up their hatchets and their assignments.

The line moved quickly. Kids chattered excitedly, shouting over the steady *chop* of hatchets against wood.

Dozens of kids had already begun work. They bent over the stumps, raising their hatchets high, chopping the stumps into splinters.

Meghan glanced around as she waited. Fallen trees lay strewn along the edges of the clearing, waiting to be carted away. The remaining stumps spread over the weeds and dirt like a small, low city. Their flat, ringed tops shone under the sparkling sunlight from above.

As Meghan reached the front of the line, a young man wearing a badge that read YOUTH CREW crossed off her name, then handed her a hatchet. Meghan grabbed the wooden handle with one hand—and nearly dropped it.

"Heavier than you thought—right?" the young man asked. "Always use two hands. These things can be dangerous." He pointed to a table behind him, surrounded by kids. "Get your work gloves over there. Find your size. Then just pick a stump."

Meghan followed his instructions. A few minutes later, she was bent over a large, round stump at the edge of the clearing, taking a few practice chops. The heavy blade sliced easily into the wood, making it seem as soft as paper.

Meghan raised the hatchet again and again, bringing it down on the edges of the stump, splintering off chunk after chunk. The *thock* of the hatchet—the *thocks* all around—made such a pleasant sound. The sunlight felt good on Meghan's face. And the splintered wood smelled sweet and fresh.

She had chopped up nearly a third of the stump and stopped to mop sweat off her forehead with a handkerchief—when a shadow fell over the ground from behind her.

She turned to see Robin Fear. He gripped a pair of tan work gloves in one hand, a hatchet in the other. He flashed her a shy smile. "Hi. I made it."

Meghan brushed a mosquito off her cheek. "Where were you?" she asked Robin. "We all started hours ago."

He sighed. "My father was all over the house. He kept wanting to talk to me and ask me questions. Maybe he suspected something. I don't know. But I couldn't get away. Finally, I sneaked out."

Meghan lowered her hatchet blade to the ground. "Robin, I'm really worried about you. If your father suspected something, won't he notice that you're missing?"

Robin scowled. "I don't care," he replied heatedly. "I'm not afraid of him." He pulled on the work gloves. "I'm going to show him that he is wrong. That he cannot control people's lives. That it's wrong to be so selfish."

He hoisted the hatchet. Meghan saw a bitter smile spread over his face. "That's my speech for the day," he said softly. "Now where should I go?"

Meghan pointed. "We can work on the same stump. Take the other side. See? I've already done a lot of it."

Robin dragged the hatchet blade across the ground as he moved around the stump. Meghan pulled up her gloves, raised the hatchet, and brought it down hard.

"See? That's how it's done," she told him.

She glanced up—and a flash of white light made her nearly drop the hatchet.

"Sorry." A young man in a gray suit and a checkered cap lowered his big camera. "I'm taking photographs for the newspaper. This is a big story in Shadyside, you know."

"We know," Robin said dryly.

"Let me get a group shot," the photographer said. He turned and shouted. "Hey, everybody—raise your hatchets and smile!"

A few minutes later, the photographer had finished. Meghan watched him lope away toward the street.

Turning back to her work, she stared into the glare of the sun. And saw somebody run up behind Robin.

Richard?

"Hey, you!" Richard called angrily.

Meghan squinted to see his face through the white glare of sunlight. But she didn't need to see him to hear his rage.

"Richard—please!" Meghan pleaded.

"I warned you to stay away from Meghan!" Richard cried.

Meghan heard Richard utter a furious growl. What was he doing? Was he raising his hatchet?

"Richard—no! *Don't!*" Meghan shrieked.

Too late.

Squinting into the white light, she saw Richard swing the hatchet at Robin. Swing it. Swing it so hard.

And slice off Robin's head.

chapter
17

"Nooooooo!"

Meghan's moan of horror rang through the trees. Her whole body shuddered. And her hatchet fell to the ground as she raised both hands to her face.

The sky darkened as a high cloud rolled over the sun. And as her eyes adjusted to the dimming light, she saw—to her relief—that she had been wrong.

Robin had sunk to his knees to avoid the swinging blade. He was okay.

"I warned you!" Richard was screaming wildly. "I warned you!"

"What's going on here?" a boy's voice called out. Meghan turned to see three or four boys, their faces tight with alarm, running toward Richard.

Robin tried to roll out of the way. But Richard, his face red with fury, raised his hatchet again.

"No!" Meghan's cry was choked off by her terror.

"Stop!" a chubby boy with short, brown hair called.

Meghan could see others running toward them. Could see their frightened, confused faces. Hear their cries.

Robin climbed to his feet. Tried to dodge away.

"Stop!" the chubby boy cried. "Don't anybody move!"

"Freeze! Everybody freeze!" a girl shouted.

"Ohh." Meghan gasped as Richard swung the hatchet again.

It made a sick *thunk* as the blade sliced deep into the chubby boy's chest.

The boy's eyes bulged in disbelief. He gazed down at the bright red blood that flowed from his body, straight down his front like a waterfall. Then he collapsed to his knees, making high whimpering sounds.

Meghan shrieked as Richard swung again. The blade caught the boy's neck and cleanly lopped off his head.

Horrified cries forced Meghan to cover her ears. She stared at the boy's head, lying facedown beside a blood-splattered stump.

When she raised her eyes, she saw another boy swing his hatchet, a two-handed blow. The blade sank into Richard's back.

Richard's hands flew up as if he wanted to take off

and fly. He uttered a hoarse bleat as another blade cut into his side.

Meghan heard Richard's final groan as his eyes turned up into his head and he sank to the dirt. Dead.

Richard. Dead.

"What is happening?" Meghan wailed. "What is happening?"

She tried to cover her eyes. But her hands wouldn't cooperate. She couldn't move. Couldn't take her eyes off the scene of horror all around her.

As hatchets swung. And kids cried out.

Startled shrieks of pain.

A blade sliced off a girl's arm at the shoulder. Meghan watched the arm slide over the blood-soaked dirt like some kind of snake.

Thock.

A red-haired boy grabbed for his knee. Too late. A hatchet blade neatly sliced off his leg.

Thock. Thock.

Shrill shrieks cut through the air as hatchet blades slashed into struggling, battling bodies.

In front of Meghan, two girls battled. Swung hard. Sent their blades deep into each other's sides.

What is happening? Meghan asked herself. She started to back up, to back away, to back toward the trees.

In front of her, she saw a frenzy of horror. Kids chopped at one another. Swung and chopped. Swung and chopped.

Until the tree stumps and the ground around them were soaked with dark blood.

Arms lay strewn in the dirt. A head rolled to a stop against a blood-smeared rock.

Meghan backed away. And as she moved back, gripped in disbelief, gripped in horror, she raised her eyes to the trees.

And saw strange, purple smoke. A purple mist floating low over the trees.

What is happening?

What is happening?

A hand grabbed Meghan's arm roughly. She cried out. Turned to see Robin.

His face was smeared with dirt. His whole body trembled. He held on to her arm as if holding himself up.

"They've all gone crazy!" He had to scream over the wails of horror and cries of pain. "It—it—it's so horrible! They're chopping each other to bits!"

Meghan opened her mouth to reply, but couldn't choke out a sound.

"Run home!" Robin screamed. "Get away from here, Meghan. Run home! Call the police! They've all gone crazy! They've just gone crazy!"

"Okay!" Meghan agreed. "Okay, Robin, I'll—"

"I'm going, too," Robin called. "I can't stand this! I can't!" He spun away and ran toward the trees.

Meghan took a deep breath. Then she started to run toward the street.

She ran past Richard's cut, blood-drenched body.

Past a work boot with a foot and leg attached. Past the table, still piled with work gloves.

I've got to run home, she told herself. Got to run. Got to run *away* from this.

But as she reached the trees, she turned back. And took one last, horrified glance at the few kids still standing, swinging their hatchets, battling each other, flailing wildly at each other, chopping one another to pieces.

As the purple smoke floated and swirled, floated and swirled around them.

chapter
18

Robin shut his eyes as he ran through the purple smoke. His heart pounded. His leg muscles ached and throbbed.

But he ran without slowing. Ran over upraised tree roots and fallen limbs. Ran between the tangled, old trees.

He knew the woods well. He had spent many hours wandering in them.

He reached the trickling stream and turned toward his house. Still running, he reached his back lawn a few minutes later. He didn't slow himself until he reached the back door.

Inside, he breathlessly called to his father. "Dad! Dad! Where are you? Dad?"

Nicholas Fear appeared in the front hallway. He

was dressed as usual in a dark business suit, white shirt, and dark necktie. He carried a book in one hand.

"Dad!" Robin wheezed. "Dad, it—it—"

"What's wrong?" Nicholas cried. "Robin, what happened? What is the matter?"

Robin took a deep breath. "Dad, it—it worked perfectly," he said. A smile spread over his face.

Nicholas narrowed his eyes at his son. "You mean . . . ?"

"They chopped each other to pieces," Robin reported, his smile growing wider. He let out a laugh. "I did everything right, Dad. And they all went wild and hacked each other up. The park will *never* be built now."

Nicholas smiled and put a hand on Robin's shoulder. "Good work, son," he said happily. "You learned your powers quickly."

"Of course," Robin replied, grinning back at his father. "I'm a Fear."

PART THREE

This Year

chapter

19

"**P**aul! Stop it!" Dierdre Bradley cried. She shoved Paul Malone with all her might. But he kept the sticky cone of pink cotton candy in her face. He let out his high-pitched giggle.

"You're not funny!" Dierdre screamed angrily, shoving him again. "Give me a break." She rubbed her cheeks with both hands. "Now I'm all sticky. You jerk. You got it in my hair."

Still giggling, Paul helped her wipe the sticky spots from her long, straight, black hair. "Leave me alone," Dierdre growled, glaring at him with her green eyes.

Then, without warning, she grabbed the paper cone from his hand and shoved the cotton candy as hard as she could into *his* face.

Startled, Paul cried out. Then they both collapsed against the side of a ticket booth, laughing, pulling the sticky goo off each other.

"We're not going to test out any rides at this rate," Dierdre complained.

Paul leaned forward and kissed her, a long, tender kiss. Then he grinned. "I don't care."

Dierdre tried to push him away. But he refused to budge. She tugged his wavy, light-brown hair with both hands till he cried out. They both laughed again.

She loved the way his blue eyes crinkled up when he laughed. He's really great-looking, she thought. She wished she cared about him a little bit more.

The way he stared at her, so lovingly, made her feel guilty.

"I'm glad I didn't take that job upstate," Paul said. He leaned forward to kiss her again.

She dodged away. "You were stupid," she told him. "You could have made twice as much money. Daddy is hardly paying you minimum wage to run the Ferris wheel."

He shrugged his broad shoulders. The silver ring in his ear caught the light from above the ticket booth. "Do I care? I get to see *you* all summer."

Dierdre felt another pang of guilt, a heavy feeling in the pit of her stomach. "Well, let's go try some rides and things," she urged.

She took his hand, which was rough, callused—he

was always building things or fiddling with cars. She tried to tug him toward the main walk of the park. But he was so much bigger than she, and so strong. She felt like a dark, little mouse beside him.

"It was really great of your dad to open the park to everyone tonight for free," Paul said. He put a heavy arm around Dierdre's shoulders and started walking slowly along the path.

"Daddy is just so excited," Dierdre replied, waving to some friends from Shadyside High. They were clustered around a dart-throwing booth, goofing around, pretending to throw darts at one another.

A group of little boys raced past happily, bursting between Dierdre and Paul. "Where is the House of Mirrors?" Dierdre heard one of them ask.

"No. Let's try the Inferno!" another boy insisted.

"Yeah! The Inferno!"

Music poured from the loudspeakers overhead. A string of red and blue lights bobbed in a soft spring breeze.

"Daddy can't believe that Fear Park is about to open next week," Dierdre continued, leaning against Paul as they walked. "It's been over sixty years. Do you *believe* it? Over sixty years since the Bradley family had the idea to build a park here."

Paul shook his head. Dierdre saw that he still had pink cotton candy stuck to the side of his nose. "Sixty years is a long time," he said. "No wonder your dad wanted to open the gates and let everyone in."

"He's just so eager for nothing to go wrong,"

Dierdre replied. "He wants to test everything before we open next week."

They turned a corner and the white lights of the Ferris wheel came into view. A line of six or seven people waited in front of it.

"Let's go on it," Paul urged, pulling Dierdre by the hand, starting to run. "You can see the whole park from the top. Actually, you can see almost all of Shadyside."

"Hey—aren't you supposed to be running it to-night?" Dierdre demanded, running to keep up with him.

He shook his head. "Wally is running it tonight. Your dad gave me the night off. To show you around, I guess."

Dierdre laughed. She swept her straight, black hair off her shoulders. "Do I need showing around? I think I know every inch of this park."

Paul nodded. He glanced at his watch. "I have to be in the Hatchet Reenactment Show at ten-fifteen," he told her. "But until then, we can do whatever we want."

The Hatchet Show.

Thinking about it always gave Dierdre a chill.

Why did her father want to replay that horrible, frightening incident every night at the park? It had happened more than sixty years ago. But the horror of it—the horror of those poor teenagers chopping and hacking one another to death—had never been forgotten by the people of Shadyside.

And now, sixty years later, Fear Park had finally

been built in the clearing where that strange and heartbreaking incident had taken place.

Dierdre's father insisted that a show in which the hatcheting was performed by actors, a vivid replay of the whole incident, was bound to be a real crowd pleaser, a major attraction.

Maybe he's right, Dierdre thought. But the whole idea had given her more than one bad dream. And when her father asked if she wanted to perform in it, she had replied, "Definitely not. No way!"

Thinking about the Hatchet Show, Dierdre climbed beside Paul in one of the shiny, new Ferris wheel seats, and felt herself being lifted toward the star-dotted sky. Halfway up, the car jerked to a stop.

Dierdre cried out, feeling herself tossed forward as the car rocked back and forth.

Paul laughed. "You know, running this thing is harder than it looks," he told her. "Other rides, you just turn them on and let them go for three or four minutes. The Ferris wheel, you've got to keep stopping it, letting people on, taking people off. There's a lot to keep track of."

Dierdre nodded. Paul kept talking, but her mind wandered.

The wheel carried them to the top. She leaned forward to peer down at all of Fear Park and the area around it. She could see the dark woods that surrounded the park. And she could make out the streetlights along Fear Street and some of the old houses there.

Paul slid his arm around her shoulders as the car

started to drop, making its slow, steady circle. She knew she should be listening to what he was saying. But she had so many other things to think about. It was hard to concentrate these days, hard to concentrate on anything.

Below, she could see people lined up for other rides, people leaning over the game booths, gathering at the food stands.

The Wild Animal Preserve wasn't open tonight. But the rest of the park was lit up and running.

Dierdre wondered where her father was. Below, she could see the long, blue trailer at the front gate that served as his office.

Please, let everything go okay tonight, she silently prayed.

Please—no accidents. No breakdowns. No problems.

Once again, the Ferris wheel jerked to a stop to let on more people. Dierdre turned and saw Paul staring at her.

"What's your problem?" he demanded.

She bit her lower lip. "Excuse me?"

"I don't think you heard a word I said," he accused.

"Oh. Uh . . ." She struggled for an excuse. "Just thinking about the park. And Daddy. You know. He's had so many problems. There have been so many weird accidents. I just want everything to go right tonight."

The car descended and stopped. Paul pushed up the safety bar and they climbed out. "Hey, Wally—

smooth ride!" he called, giving the operator a thumbs-up. "You only tossed out three riders!"

Paul and Wally laughed.

Dierdre turned and saw her father waiting for her near the exit sign. "Hey, Dee," he called.

He stepped into the light, a short, overweight man with a big paunch hanging out of his short-sleeved white shirt. He had the same black hair as Dierdre, bushy and unbrushed. He reminded Dierdre of one of the baby bears in the Wild Animal Preserve.

"How's it going, Daddy?" she asked.

Jason Bradley shrugged. "So far, so good." He had a hoarse, raspy voice. He also sounded gruff as a bear, Dierdre always thought.

She saw the dark circles around his eyes. Poor Daddy, she thought. He's aged twenty years since he took over the park for his Uncle Timothy.

"Go ride the Inferno," he ordered her, giving her a gentle push in the right direction. "Hey, Paul—you too." He tugged Paul away from Wally. "Go ride the Inferno. I want a full report—okay?"

Dierdre waved goodbye and obediently hurried with Paul to test out the Inferno. As they approached, she could hear the shrieks and cries of those already riding it.

The Inferno was the most exciting, most terrifying roller-coaster ride in Fear Park. The ride looped again and again, sending riders upside down at top speeds *six* times.

As Dierdre and Paul waited to climb on, she thought about all the trouble her father had already had with this ride. Just a week before, the scaffolding holding three painters had collapsed—seemingly for no reason at all. All three workers plunged to their deaths.

Not the first deaths. Not the first workers to die in the past sixty years, Dierdre knew.

There had been so many freak accidents. So many unexplained disasters. So many people had been killed trying to build a place where people could relax and have fun.

Dierdre shook her head hard, trying to force away the unpleasant thoughts.

She turned to see Paul grinning at her. "You scared?"

Dierdre shook her head. "You're the wimp. Not me."

"Hey!" he protested. "Who's a wimp? Come on." He tugged her along the platform. "Let's sit in the front car."

"I don't have a problem with that," Dierdre insisted.

Paul's grin grew wider. "And no hands," he added. "No holding on."

"Uh . . . okay," Dierdre agreed. What choice did she have?

The train of cars slid onto the platform, and the two of them climbed into the front seat of the front car. An attendant strapped on their safety belts, then pushed a safety bar down over their laps.

The car started slowly, clattering at first. Dierdre

leaned forward, watching the silvery tracks glide beneath them.

"No hands! No hands!" Paul reminded her.

They both raised their hands to the sky—as the car bolted sharply forward. Dierdre laughed as she felt herself tossed back hard against the plastic seat.

And then her laughter turned to a high, shrill scream as the car shot forward, looped upside down, spun and climbed. Then dipped. And climbed into another loop.

She felt the blood rush to her head. Felt her heart thud—then skip—as the car slammed her into Paul, then tilted, sending her into the other side. Then rose up as if toppling off the tracks, rose up, rose up, until they dove into another loop and swung upside down again.

"No hands! No hands!" Paul shrieked.

But Dierdre gazed over at him—and saw him clinging with both hands wrapped tightly around the safety bar.

"No hands! No hands!"

She laughed and shut her eyes as they looped upside down again.

What a great ride!

Dierdre loved it—until the car roared into the final stretch of track. Until it carried them lower, slowing, riding straight now, riding smoothly.

And Dierdre saw the metal tracks split apart up ahead.

Saw the tracks split.

Then she covered her ears. Her hands shot up to her ears as the world exploded all around her.

A deafening explosion.

It rocked the car. And shattered the tracks.

"Noooooooo!" Dierdre shrieked out her horror as the whole ride burst into a shimmering, leaping wall of orange and yellow flames.

chapter
20

"Noooooooooo!"

Dierdre covered her face with both hands as the car hurtled off the shattered tracks, carrying them into the center of the flames.

"Nooooooooo!"

The squealing wheels, the thunder of the flames, the shriek of bending metal—it all drowned out her cry.

Through the wall of fire.

Slowing, slowing.

She lowered her hands, her mouth still open, as the car eased onto the platform.

And stopped in front of the next group of people waiting to climb on.

"Please exit to your left," a recorded message repeated. "Please exit to your left."

The safety bar rose up. Dierdre unfastened the safety belt with trembling fingers. She struggled to her feet, then remembered she wasn't alone.

Stepping shakily out, she turned to Paul. He offered her a smile. But she could see the fear in his blue eyes. And he had gone as pale as the cement platform.

"Wow," he murmured, holding on to her as he climbed out. "Wow."

"Awesome finish, huh?" Dierdre said. She tried to pretend that she hadn't been scared out of her skin. "I loved it. You weren't scared too much by the fire and the explosion, were you?" she teased.

Paul swallowed hard. His blue eyes flashed. His color started to return. "Dierdre, don't try to be so cool," he scolded. "I heard you screaming. And I saw you cover your face."

"Huh? I was just trying to scare you!" Dierdre insisted.

Paul rolled his eyes. "Yeah. Right."

"Well, it's *very* real!" Dierdre declared. "I mean, when the tracks break apart and that explosion shakes the whole thing, and the fire—"

"That's why they call it the Inferno," Paul said, laughing. He grabbed her hand. "Come on. Rides like that make me hungry. Let's get some hot dogs."

Dierdre glanced at her watch. "Oh. Wow. No. I mean. I can't," she stammered.

"What's your problem?" Paul let go of her hand.

"I've . . . got to go," Dierdre replied awkwardly. "I mean, I promised Daddy. I have to help him out at the office."

Paul's face showed his disappointment. "But I thought—"

"I'll come see you at the Hatchet Show," she promised.

His mouth dropped open. "The Hatchet Show. I almost forgot. I'm supposed to rehearse." He started to back away. "Catch you later, Dee."

"Right. Later."

Dierdre turned and ran. Past the Ferris wheel. Past the long row of game booths. She turned at the end of the row and ducked into the shadows behind the last booth.

As her eyes adjusted to the darkness, she saw Rob waiting for her there, leaning against the back wall, hands shoved deep in his pockets.

He stood up as she ran toward him. Threw his arms around her. And pulled her into a long kiss.

chapter
21

"Stop," Dierdre whispered. But she kissed him again.

This is wrong, she thought. *It's so wrong.*

Why am I doing this?

"Rob, we've got to stop," she murmured, her lips against his ear. She stepped back, still gripping his hand.

His dark eyes burned into hers. He brushed back his straight, brown hair. Even in the deep shadows, she could see his intensity, his seriousness.

"It isn't fair to Paul," Dierdre whispered.

He shrugged.

Dierdre narrowed her eyes, studying him. He was shorter than Paul, not as athletic, not as good-looking.

He never bragged or got loud like Paul. He was quiet, shy. Sometimes when she was with him, he barely paid attention to her. His mind seemed to be far away. Sometimes he barely spoke to her.

So why was she here with him now?

Why was she always sneaking off to see him?

"Have you gone on any rides or anything?" Dierdre asked. Maybe chatting about something else will help take away my guilty feelings, she thought.

Poor Paul. He gave up a really good summer job to be here with me this summer. And what do I do? I . . .

Rob pulled her close and kissed her again.

I care about Paul, Dierdre thought, kissing Rob back. I know I care about Paul.

So why does Rob have such power over me?

A short while later, when Dierdre pushed open the door to her father's office trailer, she found it jammed with newspaper and TV reporters.

"Is Fear Park actually going to open next week?" a young woman in a fashionable business suit was asking Jason Bradley.

Dierdre's father beamed. "Yes, after all these years, we are finally going to open our park," he said, leaning close to the microphone in her hand.

Daddy is enjoying this, Dierdre saw. She couldn't keep a smile from spreading across her face. He already looks ten years younger, she thought.

"Why did you open the park tonight to the public for free?" the young woman asked.

Jason didn't hesitate. "I wanted everyone to see how wonderful it is," he told her. "I wanted everyone to see that this is a place the whole family can visit again and again and have a wonderful time."

"When will the Wild Animal Preserve open?" a reporter against the back wall called out.

"Next week. The preserve will open with the rest of the park," Jason told him. "It will be open only in the daytime. I would have opened it to the public tonight, but the preserve isn't lighted, so it would be hard to see the many animals we have stocked. Also, I'm still hiring staff. I don't really have enough workers to open the preserve tonight."

A tall, lanky man with curly, blond hair shoved a tape recorder into Jason's face. "Why has it taken so long to open?" he demanded. "It's been sixty years—right?"

Jason nodded, his expression turning solemn. "Yes, sixty years," he murmured sadly. "Sixty years of freak accidents. Incident after incident of unexplained tragedies. So many deaths. They kept us from building the park. It was almost as if the place was cursed. But that's all over now," he added quickly.

"The project was haunted from the start. Isn't that right?" the reporter asked.

Dierdre's father tried to smooth down his bushy, black hair. But it popped right back up over his head. He sighed.

"Yes, it started in nineteen-thirty-five. That's the

year they started to clear the land. They hired a teenaged work crew. To chop up tree stumps."

Jason frowned and lowered his eyes. "Something happened. The kids—they all went berserk. They started swinging their hatchets at each other, chopping each other up. They—"

"But *why?*" the reporter interrupted.

Jason narrowed his eyes at the man. "No one knows," he replied softly. "It's been over sixty years, and no one has a clue. The kids murdered one another. They went wild. Some kind of bizarre frenzy. Who can explain it?"

The room suddenly grew very quiet as everyone thought about that strange and terrifying scene of over sixty years before. Dierdre dropped into a folding chair. The fluorescent lights over the trailer ceiling made everyone appear pale and slightly green.

After a long, heavy silence, a young woman broke the silence. "And you've decided to act out that horrible scene every night in the park?" she demanded. Dierdre could hear the disapproval in her voice.

Jason nodded. "We're going to perform it three times a night."

"But—why?" the reporter demanded.

Jason scratched his bare arms. "Partly in tribute to the kids who died," he replied. "They died on this ground. And we don't want to forget them."

He cleared his throat. "Also, it's such a dramatic

story, such a mystery. An unsolved mystery. We know that people will be curious about it. People will want to see it. We think the Hatchet Show will become one of our biggest attractions."

A woman reporter started to ask a question. But Jason raised both hands to silence her. "The show has some wonderful special effects," he continued. "Real state-of-the-art. And we have some wonderful, hard-working young people performing in it."

He motioned to the trailer door. "I invite you all to come along with me to the show arena. You will be the first to see our Hatchet Reenactment Show."

The reporters started to file out of the trailer. As Jason passed Dierdre, he stopped and put a hand on her shoulder. "Get up. Come on," he urged. "You have to see this."

Dierdre didn't want to see it. But her father stood over her, waiting for her to join him. And she had promised Paul she would watch him perform. She really had no choice.

The night had grown cooler as she walked beside her father to the outdoor theater. Up ahead, she saw people filing in, eager to get seats.

Dierdre shivered.

Why am I dreading this show so much? she asked herself. Why do I suddenly have such a bad feeling about it?

chapter
22

Dierdre sat down beside her father in a middle row of the bleachers. The reporters and TV people squeezed around them.

Dierdre glanced around the outdoor theater. The long benches were nearly filled. More people streamed in through the entrance.

The bleachers circled the theater. They faced the center, where rows and rows of tree stumps stretched over the ground.

It really looks like a clearing in the woods, Dierdre thought. She had seen the workers building the set, but had never ventured in to take a look. Now she found herself startled at how realistic the tree stumps appeared, jutting up from the grass and weeds.

She felt a chill on the back of her neck.

Was this how the clearing looked sixty years before? Was this what those Shadyside teenagers saw—before they hacked one another to death?

Dierdre tugged down the sleeves of her sweater. She turned her attention to the crowd. She didn't want to think about what had happened on this spot. It always made her a little sick to know she was walking on the ground where such a horrible thing took place.

Red and yellow lights played over the tree stumps. Dierdre gazed at the eager, smiling faces in the audience. In the next row, two little boys were fighting over a big, stuffed bear, a prize from a game booth. Their father grabbed the bear away from them and tucked it under his arm.

"Of course we use rubber hatchets in the show," Dierdre heard her father tell a reporter. "But we spent a lot of money on the effects. It's all very real-looking, especially the blood."

He continued talking, but his voice was drowned out by three teenagers in the row above, singing a popular song at the top of their lungs.

Everyone is in such a good mood tonight, Dierdre thought. Her eyes scanned the bleachers across the theater. She recognized some of her classmates from Shadyside High.

The theater lights dimmed. Dierdre started to look away from the crowd.

But her eyes stopped on a familiar face.

She gasped as she recognized Rob.

What is *he* doing here? she asked herself. Rob said he was heading straight home. Why did he lie to me? Why did he stay for this?

She squinted, trying to see him in the dimming light. He had such a solemn expression on his face. He stared straight ahead, his features hard, his mouth set.

What is his problem? Dierdre wondered.

I'll have to ask him the next time I see him.

The crowd hushed as the lights dimmed. "I want to warn everyone that it's a pretty gruesome show," Dierdre heard her father tell the reporters. "If you're the squeamish type, you might want to hide your eyes at the end."

Dierdre rolled her eyes. She poked her father with her elbow. "Daddy," she whispered in his ear, "don't oversell it. Don't give it too big a buildup."

He grinned at her. "I'm not."

Trumpet music blared on the loudspeakers. A purple light rolled over the ground. The tree stumps shone eerily in the dark light.

Dierdre saw the performers lining up at one side of the theater. She searched for Paul. But it was too dark to see any of the actors' faces.

She wondered if Paul was nervous. He didn't want to perform in the show. He was happy manning the controls on the Ferris wheel.

But her father had forced Paul to be in the show. He liked his workers to have more than one job. It saved him money. "It's a good experience for you," Jason told Paul.

Paul couldn't argue. He didn't want to lose his Ferris wheel job. After all, he'd given up a really good job to work in the park and be close to Dierdre.

Dierdre shook those thoughts from her mind. She leaned forward, crossing her arms in front of her, and concentrated on the show.

The stumps rose under purple and blue lights as the teenagers lined up to be handed their hatchets. Dressed in work clothes of the 1930s, they chatted and laughed.

Dierdre watched them walk casually across the ground, between the rows of stumps. They all appeared happy and eager to get to work.

A taped voice on the speaker system talked about the Great Depression and told about how poor the kids were, how happy they were to be paid a dollar a day.

"Hey!" Dierdre cried out when she finally spotted Paul. He was wearing work boots, and baggy, blue denim overalls with a long-sleeved white sweatshirt underneath. His face was half hidden by a gray wool cap.

Dierdre had an urge to wave and call out to him. But she clamped her mouth shut and watched. Paul had the hatchet slung over his shoulder. He walked slowly to the center of the clearing, chatting with a girl in baggy, khaki work pants and a red bandanna.

As the announcer talked about how one hundred acres of woods had to be cleared, the performers all began to work. They circled the big tree stumps, raised their rubber hatchets, and began to hack and chop away.

Sound effects filled the theater with the heavy thud of hatchet blades and the crack of splintering wood. The kids chopped away.

Dierdre watched Paul raise his hatchet, then swing it down. His cap fell off as he raised the hatchet again, and his light brown hair tumbled over his face. Again, he brought the hatchet down, working hard.

Heavy, ominous music—low chords on an organ—rose over the sounds of chopping wood. Dierdre crossed her arms tighter against her, as if to protect herself. She knew the frightening part was about to begin.

The blue and purple lights dimmed.

A purple mist floated up over the clearing.

Where is it coming from? Dierdre wondered. Swirls of purple smoke drifted over the performers as they chopped away.

Dierdre turned to her dad. "Good smoke effect," she whispered.

He smiled, but kept his eyes straight ahead on the performance.

The solemn music grew louder as the purple smoke hovered over the clearing. The entire theater began to vibrate from the heavy chords.

Louder, louder.

Dierdre stared into the purple smoke. The workers suddenly didn't seem real. Half hidden in the smoke, they appeared to be shadows, the shadows of workers, raising their shadowy hatchets, bringing them down blindly in the thickening purple mist.

And then she saw a fight break out.

Two boys shouting angrily. She couldn't make out the words over the thunder of dark music.

But she saw the first boy swing his hatchet.

Saw it catch the other boy in the side. Saw the injured boy toss up his hands as bright red blood spurted out of his side.

And then more hatchets were swinging.

Kids screamed.

And chopped at one another.

An arm dropped to the ground.

Dierdre heard the crowd gasp. She heard cheers mixed with cries of horror, shrieks of fright.

"Great effects," a reporter leaned forward and told Dierdre's father. "Wow. So real!"

Dierdre shuddered. It's *too* real, she thought.

But she couldn't take her eyes off the horrifying scene.

Hatchets sliced into bodies. A head toppled to the ground, bounced off a blood-spattered tree stump.

The performers howled and shrieked as they went at one another, chopping and hacking, falling in agony, dying with loud cries and groans. And the dark red blood flowed over the flat stumps, between them, over the grass and weeds.

Dierdre swallowed hard. It was so gross! So gross and frightening.

She raised her eyes to the audience around her.

Saw how much they enjoyed it. Heard their cheers. Their excited cries.

When she turned back to the scene of horror, she saw Paul go down. A hatchet caught him in the back. He tossed up his hands and fell face forward over a stump.

He didn't move.

The purple mist swirled. The music droned.

As the last victim toppled to the ground, the crowd began to cheer. The purple smoke faded. The music reached a crescendo, then faded too.

The crowd applauded and cheered.

Dierdre stared at the horrifying scene, at the blood-soaked ground, at the bodies strewn all over the clearing.

So real, she thought, still hugging herself. So real. *Too* real.

She realized she *hated* the show.

It was just too ugly, too frightening.

She liked going to gross horror movies with Paul. And scary movies on TV. They didn't upset her because they weren't real.

But real kids died here, Dierdre thought. Sixty years ago, real kids chopped one another up. Not a bunch of actors.

And no one watched and applauded.

In fact, a lot of people must have cried. A lot of lives must have been ruined. A lot of families must have been shattered. A lot of tears must have fallen for months, maybe years afterward.

But now the crowd was standing, cheering, laughing, and applauding. Even the reporters had risen to applaud.

Dierdre stood up too, and watched the performers climb to their feet to take their bows.

They looked so terrible, picking themselves up from the ground, many of them appearing to have an arm or leg missing. All of them smeared with red dye, or whatever they used for blood.

One by one, they climbed to their feet and formed a line. Bowing, accepting the wild cheers of the audience.

One by one. Except for Paul.

Paul?

Dierdre stared at his unmoving body, sprawled over a tree stump, hands dangling to the ground.

Not moving. Not moving.

"Paul?" she screamed. "Paul?"

Without even realizing it, she began running down the bleacher aisle, running onto the clearing. Arms outstretched. Screaming as she ran.

"Paul? Get up, Paul! Get up!"

chapter
23

Dierdre caught the startled glances of the performers as she burst into the clearing. She heard gasps from the crowd.

Did they finally see that Paul wasn't getting up?

"Paul? Paul? Are you okay?"

Her sneakers slid in a puddle of dark red dye and she nearly fell right on top him.

"Paul? Paul?"

He turned toward her, his features tight with pain, and groaned.

"Paul—what's wrong?" Dierdre demanded shrilly. "What happened?"

He opened his mouth. But only another groan came out.

He sucked in a deep breath. "Cramp in my side," he finally choked out.

Dierdre's mouth dropped open. "Huh?"

"Cramp in my side," Paul repeated, sounding a little stronger. "I think I pulled a muscle when I fell onto the stump."

Dierdre let out a long sigh. "Oh, wow. I thought . . ." Her voice trailed off. She wasn't sure *what* she thought.

Rubbing his side, Paul hoisted himself to his feet.

The crowd applauded. He took a bow. Everyone laughed.

"This show is *dangerous!*" Paul declared, grinning at her.

"Are you okay?" she asked, her heart still pounding.

He nodded.

She threw her arms around his shoulders and kissed him.

And over his shoulder she saw a face. A face in the audience. A face she knew.

Rob's face. Staring hard at them. Not blinking. Not moving.

Watching them.

chapter
24

"**D**addy, I don't *believe* you!" Dierdre cried. "Wasn't *one* free sneak preview enough?"

Jason Bradley turned from the stack of papers on his desk. He looked pale and drawn. But he grinned at Dierdre and shrugged his broad shoulders.

"It went so well last night," he said. His chubby fingers thumped the desktop. "I'm still excited. Look at me, Dee. I can't calm down."

"And so . . .?" Dierdre started.

"So I had to open up the park again tonight. I'm too wired to sit around and wait till next week. One more sneak preview. One more free night for the public. Did you see the news stories on TV?"

Dierdre nodded. "Yes, I saw the stories. I was

141

home with you, remember? We watched them together."

"Oh. Yeah. Right." Jason raked a hand back
through his bushy hair. "You see how crazed I am? I
don't even remember my own daughter!"

They both laughed. Dierdre stepped up behind
him and gave him a hug.

"I know how happy you are, Daddy," she said
tenderly. "I'm happy, too. After so many years and
so many problems, your dream is finally coming
true."

When he turned to her, Jason had tears in his eyes.
"Now it's going so well," he said. "After last night, I
knew we were finally okay."

Dierdre hugged him again. She glanced at the
clock on his desk. "Oh. Wow. I've got to run. I
promised Paul I'd meet him by the front gate before
the park opened."

"Tonight is Paul's first night running the Ferris
wheel," her father said, turning back to his papers.

"He's very excited about it," Dierdre told him.
"He likes it better than getting hatcheted in the back
and having to throw himself over a tree stump."

Jason laughed. "Who wouldn't?"

Dierdre ran out of the trailer. The door slammed
shut behind her.

She stepped into a cool, gray evening, a pale
crescent moon just rising over the trees beyond the
park. She took a deep breath, inhaling the sweet
aroma of cotton candy and freshly popped popcorn.

Park workers scurried to their places. The park

was scheduled to open in about twenty minutes for its second night free to the public.

Dierdre shook her head, thinking about her father and how out of control he was. He's totally lost it, she told herself.

And she was glad.

Her smile dimmed as Rob popped into her mind.

She had called him at his house earlier in the afternoon. He sounded very surprised to hear from her.

"I saw you last night. At the Hatchet Show," Dierdre had told him.

"Oh. Yeah. Right," he had stammered awkwardly.

"How come you went?" Dierdre demanded. "You told me you were going straight home."

"It looked interesting, that's all," Rob replied. "I was passing by, and I saw everyone going in. So I went in, too."

"But you had such a serious look on your face—" Dierdre started. "I thought—"

"I didn't know what to expect," Rob cut in. "I mean, I didn't know the story or anything. Then when everyone started swinging their hatchets, and it got so bloody—I guess I was upset or something. I couldn't believe it. I mean, all those heads being chopped off and—"

"It's really gross, isn't it?" Dierdre commented.

"Yeah," Rob agreed. "I—I can't believe it really happened. I mean, how can that be a true story?"

They chatted a while longer about the park. As they talked, Dierdre's feelings of guilt returned. Paul cared about her so much. He had even talked about them choosing a college together so they wouldn't be separated when they graduated from Shadyside High.

She liked Paul, too. She liked him a lot.

So why was she so drawn to Rob?

Why had she been sneaking off with this boy she knew so little about?

"Can I see you later? At the park?" Rob had asked on the phone that afternoon.

"Uh . . . well . . ." Dierdre hesitated. "I don't think so," she replied finally. "I'm meeting Paul before the gates open. And then—"

"Paul, Paul, Paul," Rob had murmured.

"Excuse me?" Dierdre cried.

"I've got to get off," Rob said sharply. "Maybe I'll see you later."

"But I already told you. I'm meeting Paul and—"

"Later," Rob insisted. And hung up.

Now Dierdre's eyes searched the main gate for Paul. Not there. The ticket takers were entering the small, round booths. Dierdre guessed they were just practicing. No tickets were needed tonight. The park was free.

Dierdre paced back and forth for a few minutes. Where *is* he? she wondered. The park is about to open. He should have been here a while ago.

Maybe we got our signals crossed, she decided.

Maybe he thought I'd meet him at the Ferris wheel.

Yes. That makes sense. Paul has to be on duty there. He's probably waiting for me.

Dierdre turned and started to jog toward the rides area. She passed her father's trailer office and kept running. A few seconds later, she turned a corner onto the main walkway.

The Ferris wheel, white lights blazing its outline, came into view.

Weird, Dierdre thought, jogging past a row of game booths. Paul has the wheel already turning. He didn't wait for the park to open.

Maybe he's just giving it a practice spin, she thought. The lights look so beautiful against the evening sky.

"Oh!" Dierdre cried out, and stopped running, when she noticed something strange about the spinning Ferris wheel.

It wasn't spinning smoothly.

It bumped. The cars rocked back and forth.

She watched it spin for a few seconds. Then bump. Spin. Then bump.

Is it broken? she wondered. Why is it doing that?

Does Paul realize that the wheel is spinning so raggedly?

Keeping her eyes on the wheel, Dierdre ran the rest of the way. "Hey, Paul? Paul? Are you here?" she shouted, running up the narrow path on the side that led up to the control panel.

"Paul?"

No one at the controls.

She spun back to the wheel. Why was it going with no one at the control panel?

The big wheel spun. Then bumped. Spun. Then bumped.

Dierdre heard a soft *thud* each time it bumped.

She took a few steps toward the wheel. Then stopped.

And stared under the wheel. Under the wheel.

At the shoes under the wheel. The legs.

Under the wheel. What *was* under the wheel?

She took another step. Stared harder.

Then started to scream.

chapter

25

Paul's head had been neatly sliced off. It lay on its side on the pavement, wide-eyed, light-brown hair matted down, the open throat emptying out onto the walk.

Gasping for breath, her hands pressed against her cheeks, Dierdre forced herself to turn away from it.

And once again, she saw Paul's body jammed under the wheel. The shoes poking out. The legs. The rest of Paul.

Bump. Bump.

The legs and shoes jumped up as each car bumped over the body.

As if alive, Dierdre thought. The shoes keep jumping—*as if Paul is alive!*

Bump. Bump.

Paul's body made the big wheel skip. Slide, then skip. Each car tilted and rocked as it bumped over what was left of him.

"Nooooooo!" Dierdre wailed. "Nooooooo. Not Paul. Not Paul!"

She watched the shoes jump up one more time.

Then she staggered away, tears blinding her, burning her eyes.

A figure hurried up to meet her.

Rob!

He wrapped his arms around her. Held her tightly, trying to stop her sobs, her trembling, her tears.

"It's okay, Dee," Rob whispered tenderly. Leading her away. Leading her away from the horror. "It's okay. I'm here now. I'll take care of you, Dee. I'll take good care of you now."

"When will the park open, Daddy?" Dierdre asked as her father stepped out of the office trailer.

Two weeks later. And the police still covered the park, investigating Paul's strange death.

An accident? Murder?

The park couldn't open until the question was answered.

Jason shrugged wearily. Just looking at him made Dierdre feel sad. All the life had drained from his eyes. He hunched his shoulders as he walked, like an old man.

Like a defeated man.

He had come so close to his dream. And now another tragedy had delayed it—maybe forever.

He sighed. "The police think maybe we can open in a few weeks," he told her, speaking so faintly she could barely hear him.

"That's good news," Dierdre replied, trying to sound cheerful.

"But a lot of the workers quit," Jason said, shaking his head. "They said Fear Park is jinxed. They don't want to work here. I have no one for the food stands. No one to work half the games. No one to run the Ferris wheel . . ."

"I think I could do that." A voice broke into their conversation.

Dierdre turned to see Rob standing beside her. His dark hair was carefully brushed. He wore a dark tie over a pale-blue shirt.

He's applying for a job, Dierdre realized.

She saw her father eye Rob suspiciously.

"This is Rob," she said quickly. "He's a friend of mine, Daddy."

Jason's expression softened a bit. "Rob?"

Rob nodded shyly. "Well, actually," he offered reluctantly, "my name is Robin. Robin Fear, sir."

Jason's eyes widened in surprise. "A Fear?" he demanded sharply. "Are you related to the Fear family?"

Robin shrugged. "I think I'm a distant cousin," he told Dierdre's father. "I'm really not sure."

Jason studied him carefully. "And you think you can operate the Ferris wheel?"

Robin nodded. His dark eyes flashed excitedly.

"Oh, yes, sir," he replied. "I'll try my best, Mr. Bradley. I'll work really hard."

Dierdre saw a strange smile spread over Robin's face. "I've waited a *long* time for this job!" he exclaimed.

TO BE CONTINUED . . .

About the Author

"Where do you get your ideas?"

That's the question that R. L. Stine is asked most often. "I don't know where my ideas come from," he says. "But I do know that I have a lot more scary stories in my mind that I can't wait to write."

So far, he has written nearly five dozen mysteries and thrillers for young people, all of them bestsellers.

Bob grew up in Columbus, Ohio. Today he lives in an apartment near Central Park in New York City with his wife, Jane, and son, Matt.

THE NIGHTMARES
NEVER END . . .
WHEN YOU VISIT

Next . . .
FEAR PARK #2
THE LOUDEST SCREAM
(Coming mid-August 1996)

Every day something horrible happens at Fear Park. Dierdre Bradley is starting to believe that the amusement park her father owns *is* cursed. The only good thing in Dierdre's life is her new boyfriend, Robin Fear.

But Dierdre doesn't know that sixty years ago Robin found a spell to make himself immortal—so he could make sure that Fear Park never opens. He'll do anything to destroy the amusement park. Even kill Dierdre.

Now your younger brothers or sisters
can take a walk down Fear Street....

R·L·STINE'S
GHOSTS of FEAR STREET°

1 Hide and Shriek	52941-2/$3.99
2 Who's Been Sleeping in My Grave?	
	52942-0/$3.99
3 Attack of the Aqua Apes	52943-9/$3.99
4 Nightmare in 3-D	52944-7/$3.99
5 Stay Away From the Treehouse	52945-5/$3.99
6 Eye of the Fortuneteller	52946-3/$3.99
7 Fright Knight	52947-1/$3.99
8 The Ooze	52948-X/$3.99
9 Revenge of the Shadow People	52949-8/$3.99
10 The Bugman Lives	52950-1/$3.99
11 The Boy Who Ate Fear Street	00183-3/$3.99

A MINSTREL® BOOK

Simon & Schuster Mail Order
200 Old Tappan Rd., Old Tappan, N.J. 07675
Please send me the books I have checked above. I am enclosing $_____ (please add
$0.75 to cover the postage and handling for each order. Please add appropriate sales
tax). Send check or money order—no cash or C.O.D.'s please. Allow up to six weeks
for delivery. For purchase over $10.00 you may use VISA: card number, expiration
date and customer signature must be included.

POCKET
B O O K S

Name _____

Address _____

City _____ State/Zip _____

VISA Card # _____ Exp.Date _____

Signature _____

1180-07

FEAR STREET® SAGA

Collector's Edition

Including
The Betrayal
The Secret
The Burning

R·L·STINE

Why do so many terrifying things happen on Fear Street? Discover the answer in this special collector's edition of the *Fear Street Saga* trilogy, something no Fear Street fan should be without.

Special bonus: the Fear Street family tree, featuring all those who lived—and died—under the curse of the Fears.

Coming in mid-October 1996

From Archway Paperbacks
Published by Pocket Books

POCKET
B O O K S

1233

FEAR STREET® SAGA

...WHERE THE TERROR BEGAN

R.L. STINE

The Betrayal

*Why do so many horrifying things happen on Fear Street?
Nora knows.*

❏ 86831-4/$3.99

The Secret

*What is the secret of Fear Street? Why has its
horror lasted for so long?*

❏ 86832-2/$3.99

The Burning

*Simon Fear thought changing his name
would stop the evil. He was wrong—dead wrong.*

❏ 86833-0/$3.99

An Archway Paperback
Published by Pocket Books

Simon & Schuster Mail Order
200 Old Tappan Rd., Old Tappan, N.J. 07675
Please send me the books I have checked above. I am enclosing $_____ (please add $0.75 to cover the postage
and handling for each order. Please add appropriate sales tax). Send check or money order–no cash or C.O.D.'s
please. Allow up to six weeks for delivery. For purchase over $10.00 you may use VISA: card number, expiration
date and customer signature must be included.

Name _____

Address _____

City _____ State/Zip _____

VISA Card # _____ Exp.Date _____

Signature _____ 1181